A Brazen Bride

Monica Marks

Published by Trellis Publishing, 2021.

A BRAZEN BRIDE

First edition. July 9, 2021.

Copyright © 2021 Monica Marks.

ISBN: 979-8224441679

Written by Monica Marks.

THE BRAZEN BRIDE

MONICA MARKS

The Colville siblings stood at the end of the road, both lost in their own thoughts. The heat was becoming almost unbearable in the afternoon sun but Lucille lowered her fan to stare at the house before casting her brother a small smile. It lacked mirth and it mirrored what Nicholas was feeling.

"Well, it is not much, is it?" she laughed, using the fan again to sweep air over her fair face, causing her dark hair to shift along the lines of her yellow bonnet. "Uncle Charles was not one for upkeep although I cannot say I am surprised, given his age."

"We will make it liveable yet," Nicholas replied, a note of defensiveness touching his words. Their uncle had only just passed and they had not known of his demise until word had come from a solicitor in Cheyenne. The man had bequeathed his farm to the siblings, Charles' only known relatives.

Nicholas was ten years his sister's senior and had fond memories of the odd old man who had been his father's brother. Lucille could not possibly remember when Charles had lived in Pennsylvania before making his way toward Wyoming where he had found his own land. Charles had never married nor sired any children of his own, making his brother's children the heirs to the dilapidated estate.

Nicholas had to admit his sister was correct—their uncle had not done much to sustain the vast property with its crumbling house structure and overgrown gardens but there was livestock, cows, chickens and a few horses from what he had gleaned. There was a profit to be made if only they had the motivation to work.

It needs only a modicum of care and we will be fruitful here.

Matters had been dire in following the death of their father, five years earlier, James Colville's debts nearly breaking the siblings financially. James had lived well beyond his means and it had been up to Nicholas to make good on his father's overspending. Charles' gift had come at a seemingly sound moment as Nicholas prepared to sell their lavish home in Pittsburgh.

"Praise the Lord the Hovingtons are nearby," Lucille sighed, stepping gingerly toward the house. She squealed as her foot touched the mud and Nicholas laughed at her histrionics.

"It is not a bit like the city, is it?" she mumbled almost angrily but Nicholas was thinking about what Lucille had said about their friends in the nearby city.

The Hovingtons had emigrated from England with Lucille and Nicholas' parents thirty years prior and while James Colville had done well for himself as a banker in Pennsylvania, the Hovingtons had continued to chase the dream of owning land by heading west two decades earlier.

They lived an hour away in Cheyenne with their daughter, Chasity and that was precisely where Nicholas' mind focussed.

He did not much remember the girl of one who had headed west with her parents when he was a boy of seven but Nicholas knew she was of good breeding and would make a decent wife. The Godfrey Hovington, Chasity's father, had already agreed to the nuptials through letter. It was only a matter of asking for the young woman's hand.

Lucille and I will fix this land to its original splendor and I will send word to Chasity that she and I will be married, Nicholas thought with pleasure. Despite the setbacks that he and his sister had faced, Nicholas was certain that the future was bright for them both.

God bless Uncle Charles for this generous gift and keep his soul. We will not squander it. We will make it a home and generations of Colvilles will continue to seed their roots on the land.

"You are thinking of Chasity, are you not?"

"I am," Nicholas replied to his sister. "What of it?"

"When will you propose?"

Nicholas waved his hands about to indicate the work which needed to be done.

"As soon as we make this land presentable for a lady," he replied cheekily and Lucille giggled.

"I daresay we best get it in order then," she replied, closing her fan and tucking it into her small purse. "I would rather have nephews and nieces in this lifetime."

~ ~ ~

It took two months for the Colvilles to fix the damage which had befallen their uncle's ranch home but with the tenacity which had been bred in them, the siblings worked tirelessly and managed to bring the property into a decent state of repair. Nicholas knew that the speed in which they had accomplished the task was directly related to the betrothal weighing on his mind.

He had visited the Hovingtons twice since their arrival, walking with Chasity both times after their evening meal and while she was hardly a stimulating girl, he was more certain than ever that she would make him a decent match.

Her family was well-off and her dowry only added to the benefits of wedding her. What did it matter that Chasity seemed more consumed with fashion than the details of running the ranch? Surely she would adjust once she was faced with the task upon arriving at the Colville's new home.

It was only then that Nicholas sat at his writing desk in the breezy study and began to pen a letter.

My Dearest, it began. *I will keep this letter short and to the directive. I feel the time has come for us to be wed. The ranch is now functioning well and in need of more hands to ensure its operation. I would prefer the nuptials occur sooner than later. I await your response. Nicholas Colville*

He felt that he had waited long enough without trusting the mails to deliver the proposal and Nicholas sent for a messenger to deliver the letter.

"I would like a response immediately," Nicholas told the messenger. "Return to me at once with an answer."

"Yes, sir."

He watched as the boy disappeared on horseback, leaving Nicholas smiling with satisfaction.

"Have you swallowed a bird?" Lucille chirped.

"I have sent off my proposal to Miss Chasity," he informed his sister. "I await a reply."

Lucille clapped her white gloves together in glee and smiled broadly.

"Oh happy day!" she sang. "I will finally have help!"

"And I will have a wife," Nicholas replied, contented.

~ ~ ~

By sundown, the messenger had returned. Nicholas washed at the well as Lucille prepared the evening meal.

Nicholas whirled when he heard the sound of hooves approaching.

"Well?" he asked eagerly, hurrying toward the page. "What did she say?"

He nodded stiffly but Nicholas could see the twinkle in his eye.

"She said she would be honored to oblige your request, Mr. Colville and she will tell you so in person."

Nicholas' face twisted into a smile and relief flooded his body. He had been certain she would agree to the marriage but the anticipation had left him tense.

The page turned on his horse but before he left, he cast Nicholas a look over his shoulder.

"She is quite a comely lass," he muttered, seeming embarrassed that he needed to say so. "I have never seen so much woman."

Nicholas' brow furrowed, less because of the bold statement by a messenger boy but by the assessment of Chasity Hovington. She was attractive enough but comely was not a word Nicholas would have used to describe her. He would likely not have noticed her on the street if he did not know her.

The page mistook Nicholas' frown for that of disapproval and muttered an apology before kicking his horse and speeding away.

Odd boy, Nicholas thought but he did not push the issue. He was filled with a deep sense of satisfaction. After the trials life had bestowed upon him, things were finally progressing as he had expected.

"Will you stand out here all night or will you come and eat the meal I have so laboriously prepared?"

Lucille appeared at his side and Nicholas nodded.

"I am coming," he told her, smiling warmly. "I have received word that I will be married and soon you will have someone to share the chores."

"Miss Chasity has agreed then?"

"Indeed," Nicholas murmured happily and Lucille squealed.

"How wonderful! I have always longed for a sister."

Nicholas followed his younger sibling toward the house, warmth flooding him as he thought of the days ahead.

~ ~ ~

No sooner had the siblings sat down to eat did a loud knock startle them both.

"Who could that be at the dinner hour?" Lucille asked as Nicholas rose to respond.

"I will send whoever it is away," her brother replied, stalking toward the front door purposefully.

Yet when he pulled on the handle, he was taken aback but the woman he saw, his jaw falling slightly.

She was flame-haired with eyes of blazing green and adorned a frayed, working dress of drab brown. Her mass of curls was not even contained beneath a kerchief, let alone a bonnet and her hands were filthy.

None of this did distract from the voluptuous form of her body which threatened to bust from the seams of her attire.

"May I help you?" Nicholas asked, his brow knitting in curiosity and slight contempt. He suspected she was a gypsy, seeking work and prepared to close the door on her face but to his utter shock, she stepped across the threshold and threw her arms about his neck.

Nicholas reeled back, stunned at the brazenness of her action.

"Unhand me!" he managed to gasp as he wriggled out of her grasp. "What is the meaning of this?"

Her face broke into a stunningly white smile and she cocked her head to look at him.

"It's me, Nicky. Faith," she replied.

"I-I do not know you!" he protested, again stepping back as though worried she might try again to touch him. "You must have the wrong property."

She shook her mane of unruly red curls and reached into the folds of her ripe bosom.

"I think not," she replied, a lilting note to her voice. Nicholas watched in horrified fascination as she withdrew a page from her breast and flapped it in his face.

"What is the meaning of this?" Lucille asked, apparently attracted by the commotion. "Who is this, Nicholas?"

But he was far too transfixed by the letter Faith held and his heart caught in his throat.

"I am Nicky's betrothed," the fire-haired tart called. "See? He has proposed marriage to me and I have accepted."

Ire sparked through Nicholas, his face flushing red.

"That letter was clearly not meant for you!" he growled, reaching forward to snatch it from her. He wondered how the messenger had gotten confused.

"It was!" Faith insisted. "It was addressed to my home."

"Give that to me at once!" Nicholas snapped but Faith darted away, shaking her head.

"I will not. It is mine now. When we are married, what is mine will be yours, however."

Nicholas looked at his sister, his mouth agape. His inkling was to laugh at such a display but his sense of anger and pride overtook any amusement.

"Have you taken leave of your senses?" he demanded, snorting in contempt. "Off with you, woman. "

He moved to shove her from the threshold but as he did, she unleashed an earth-shattering scream which curdled his blood.

"Is this any way to treat your betrothed!" she screamed. "I will not leave!"

She stomped her foot for effect and Nicholas was at a loss for words.

He looked helplessly at his sister again but Lucille seemed transfixed with what was happening and did not meet his eyes.

"You are not my betrothed!" Nicholas rasped, his words escaping in short, uneven bouts. "You are mad if you think you are!"

"You are without honor if you do not marry me!" Faith retorted, again waving the letter in his face. "What kind of gentleman would you be if you did not grace your promises?"

Nicholas threw up his hands in disgust and turned to his sister.

"You must rid her from this house. I fear I will lose my wits if I am forced to deal with her another moment!"

With that, he strode away from the women and retreated into the dining room where he plopped heavily into his chair but suddenly, he realized he was no longer hungry.

She is daft! How could she possibly believe that the letter was meant for her?

Nicholas realized he would need to find the messenger and see how matters had gone so terribly awry but that would need to wait until morning. The hour was late and he was exhausted from the day's events.

He trusted that his sister would aptly remove the obnoxious woman from his land but when Lucille appeared a few minutes later, he sensed that the red-haired devil was still nearby.

"She will not leave," Lucille sighed. "Perhaps you should offer her something to make her go away."

"Money?" Nicholas scoffed. "I will not succumb to common extortion! I will fetch the law if need be!"

Lucille perched gingerly on the edge of a chair and leaned forward with worried blue eyes.

"Nicholas, I fear you may be in the wrong here. You addressed the letter only to 'My Dearest' and the lettering is so smudged on the post, I daresay you might have placed the destination incorrectly. She may make things worse if you do not offer her a sum."

Nicholas had never heard of such a thing, a woman demanding marriage or money.

"I will do no such thing!" he said firmly. "She will leave when she sees I cannot be bent to her will. Let us eat."

"Nicholas—"

"Enough on the matter, Lucille. She will leave one way or another but it will not be with my money lining her pockets."

Lucille sat back, gingerly reclaiming her fork without a word but Nicholas could sense she had much to say on the matter still.

She is a flimflam artist, nothing more. This will pass when she sees I am not a decent target for her treachery.

~ ~ ~

Nicholas proved to be a poor prophet and in the morning when he woke, he found Faith asleep on the front stoop as though she was a feral cat.

"My word!" he choked when he stepped outside. "How dare you?"

She blinked lazily and stretched her pale arms, causing another tear in her already ill-fitting clothes.

"Good morning, my love," she chirped like there was nothing unusual about sleeping in the dirt. "Shall I make breakfast?"

Nicholas scowled, his face crimson with anger.

"You will leave before I involve the Sheriff," he growled. He did not wish to involve the law but the woman was leaving him little choice in the matter. Nicholas hoped she would not make matters more difficult than need be.

"And what would you tell the Sheriff?" she demanded, the smile dropping from her face. "That you promised to marry me and recanted? What will the townsfolk say?"

Nicholas bristled. The last thing he and Lucille needed was a scandal when they were so new to the area.

What will the Hovingtons say if they learn of this woman claiming I offered to marry her? No, I cannot permit this ridiculousness to leave the property.

Lucille's words flooded back into his mind and he gritted his teeth together.

"How much will it take to have you leave?" he asked, furious that he had relented to this woman. "I will pay it and we will be done with this."

She rose to her full, Amazonian height and shook her head. Even as tall as she was, Nicholas still did tower over her slightly.

"I have told you what it is I want—for you to honor your vow to marry me."

Nicholas groaned aloud.

"Woman, you do not know me from Adam. Why on God's earth would you wish to marry a man you do not know?"

"I will make you a decent wife," Faith told him, ignoring his question. "I can cook, clean, sew—"

"You will not force your way into this house! I have another in mind to marry!"

"And yet it is me who stands before you."

Nicholas felt a newly familiar sense of frustration mounting in him.

"It is out of the question," he told her firmly. "I can offer you money, nothing more. You may consider my terms."

He stormed past her as he moved to tend to the ranch but when he reached the barn, he could not resist casting her a look over his shoulder and inexplicably, Nicholas felt a pang of compassion for the bold stranger.

She remained in place, staring down at her hands, seeming dejected.

This is what she wants. She wishes you to feel sympathy for her and give into her ludicrous demands.

But Nicholas would not be fooled. He would rid himself of the trouble this Faith had caused and propose to Chasity again—in the flesh.

~ ~ ~

The day was consumed with chores as always and Nicholas worked tirelessly but in the back of his mind was Faith and where she was. He did not trust her to be running amok through the house but he knew Lucille would not permit her to be alone.

The west is indeed a suspicious place, Nicholas thought grimly as he baled hay. *I was warned before we left Pennsylvania but now I see that the people have few scruples. Lucille and I need be extra cautious.*

At midday, he returned to the house and when he entered, he blinked in surprise. He had never seen the interior so clean.

"Lucille?" he called. "Are you here?"

His sister appeared, wiping her hands on an apron, her eyes wide.

"I am here, Nicholas. What is it?"

He gestured around the spotless entryway.

"You have cleaned well," he commented. "And what have you for lunch? It smells delicious."

Lucille blushed furiously and darted her eyes away.

"Thank you," she mumbled. "Food will be ready soon."

Nicholas nodded and followed her into the kitchen but he froze when he saw Faith inside.

"What is she doing here?" he yelled. "Out of my house!"

"Nicholas, be calm. Faith is merely helping me while she remains."

"While she remains?" he echoed in disbelief. "She will not remain here! I will throw you out myself if I must!"

Faith was unperturbed by his outburst and continued to move easily through the kitchen, attending to the afternoon meal as though he was not even there.

"She is the one who cleaned so thoroughly," Lucille whispered, seeming embarrassed by the confession. "I admit, I rather enjoy the company."

Nicholas could not believe what he was hearing, his sister siding with a flimflam artist who deigned to take both their money.

"What lies has she fed you?" he demanded, watching the full-figured redhead glide gracefully through the room. Nicholas could not help himself from studying her form admiringly before he caught himself.

"Nicholas, I do not believe she means us harm," Lucille told him quietly. "I suspect she is seeking sanctuary."

Nicholas scoffed.

"She cannot stay here, Lucille," he said loudly enough for Faith to hear. "I do not care what her reasons are for being here."

Faith looked up at him then, her emerald eyes shadowing slightly as she stared at him.

"I fear we have reached an impasse then," she replied coldly. "For I am not going anywhere."

"This is ridiculous!" Nicholas barked. "I will not stand for such insolence in my own home."

"This is my home also," Lucille said. "And I am happy to have the help."

"You will have all the help you need when Miss Chasity arrives!" Nicholas exploded, his head swimming. "But she cannot come here while this one remains!"

He did not permit Lucille an opportunity to answer as he stormed from the house. He was no longer hungry, the situation with Faith again churning his stomach.

Yet as he left the house, he could not help but admire her attention to detail. There was not a speck of dust anywhere his eyes could see.

It matters not, he growled to himself. *She must go.*

~ ~ ~

But Faith did not go.

She remained on the Colville's property, cleaning and cooking for a week. In spite of his earlier misgivings, Nicholas found himself looking forward to the meals she made. The woman was a much better cook than his sister and while he still did not trust Faith, he begrudgingly admitted that the ranch ran much more smoothly since her arrival.

Lucille had granted her one of the servants' rooms at the back of the house and found her decent clothes to wear but Nicholas pretended not to notice how lovely she looked in the dresses of blue and green.

Faith no longer insisted he marry her but the request hung in the air and Nicholas wondered if she sincerely intended to remain until he agreed. She was not being paid for her services, aside from room and board but that did not appear to trouble Faith in the least.

One afternoon, the siblings went to town for supplies, leaving Faith back at the ranch. It was the first time they had left her unattended and Nicholas was somewhat nervous. He wondered what they would find when they returned.

"Oh!" Lucille gasped worriedly causing Nicholas to look where she did. His face paled dramatically.

"Nicholas!" Godfrey Hovington called from across the way. "There you are!"

The siblings exchanged a look and immediately forced small smiles on their faces.

"Good day, sir," Nicholas said as the older gentleman approached. "How do you fare?"

"I would be much better if I could answer when I might expect to announce your engagement to my daughter," he replied without preamble. Nicholas cringed at the words but he maintained the beam on his face.

"I did not wish to bring Miss Chasity to the house until we are quite certain it is ready for a lady of her standing," Nicholas replied quickly, hoping his sister would not undermine his fib.

"That is nonsense!" Godfrey announced. "The purpose of a wife is to ensure that the house is made into a home. You have put this off long enough. I know Chasity anxiously awaits your proposal."

Oh dear Lord, Nicholas thought, his heart fluttering. *How can I possibly explain this dilemma to him?*

"You do still intend to marry my daughter, do you not?" Godfrey demanded and to Nicholas' shock, he found himself unable to answer.

In his mind, he saw Faith working dutifully to better his life without complaint. He envisioned her sparkling green eyes and wry, jesting smile as she prepared his favorite meals, ones she had learned without him saying a word.

"Nicholas!"

"Yes, sir," Nicholas managed to choke. "Of course."

Godfrey's scowl relaxed into a smile.

"Good. Now do not delay the matter any more. I am growing weary of having so many women in my house. Good day."

With that, he was off, leaving the Colvilles to stare after him.

"You do still intend to marry Miss Chasity, do you not?" Lucille asked him but her tone suggested she sensed her brother's reluctance.

"Of course," he said again and he hoped there was conviction in his voice. "Who else would I marry?"

Lucille chuckled but she did not respond and Nicholas wondered if his sentiments were clearer to her than they were to himself.

~ ~ ~

When they returned from town, Faith was not in the house.

"Where could she have gone now?" Lucille murmured, a slight frown on her face. "All the horses are present."

A twinge of alarm touched Nicholas at the question but as they searched the property, they found no trace of her.

"Her belongings remain in her room," Lucille told him and Nicholas' alarm grew into fear. Since Faith had arrived, she had not once left the property, not even for a moment.

"Something is amiss," he told his sister. "She has befallen danger."

Lucille eyed him warily.

"Or perhaps she simply realized that you will never marry her and moved along to find another husband," she offered weakly but Nicholas could tell there was no certainty in her voice. Surely if that was so, she would have taken her sparse belongings, her toiletries, her clothes. She had even left the letter which Nicholas had written to Chasity.

"We must not jump to conclusions," Lucille said firmly. "She may simply have gone for a walk."

Yet Nicholas knew his sister did not believe her words any more than he did and as they retreated outside to look at the vast Wyoming landscape, neither spoke a word.

In their hearts, they both knew that Faith was in trouble.

~ ~ ~

Faith did not return that evening, nor was she there the following morning and when Nicholas woke from a restless sleep, he saddled his horse.

"Where are you going?" Lucille asked, hurrying toward him as he mounted Scout. "There is work to be done."

He looked at her and instantly, Lucille seemed to understand. She lowered her eyes and nodded.

"Be prepared that she may not wish to return, Nicholas. She still may have left on her own accord."

He had considered that but he refused to believe it, not under the circumstances.

"I will be back as soon as possible."

Scout snorted and the two moved off toward the horizon in the way of town. His first order of business was finding the messenger who had delivered the letter to Faith.

He found the boy in town and when Nicholas approached, the page recognized him instantly.

"Mr. Colville! Have you been married, sir?"

"I have a bone to pick with you, boy!" Nicholas growled. "Where did you deliver that letter?"

The messenger blinked in confusion and shook his head.

"To the Hovington residence in Wyoming as instructed," he replied without hesitation. "I handed it to the lady herself."

"A flame-haired woman? She claimed to be Miss Chasity Hovington?"

"She was not?"

Nicholas groaned inwardly, realizing that his task was becoming much more difficult than he anticipated. If Faith had been a servant in the Hovington household who had simply interceded the message, that meant that Nicholas would need to return to the Hovingtons to find her and that would rouse questions he was not prepared to answer.

Yet what choice did he have but to go? He doubted very much that Faith had returned to whatever her position may have been at the Hovingtons but there was nowhere else to check for her.

The sense that she was in danger did not diminish as he guided Scout the hour ride into Wyoming where he found himself at the door of the Hovingtons, a maidservant announcing his arrival to the household.

Godfrey appeared, a jovial grin touching his moustached lips.

"Ah, Nicholas!" he called cheerfully. "I shall fetch Chasity. I assume that is why you have come?"

"Do not," Nicholas said firmly, causing the beam to slip from Godfrey's mouth. "I have come to speak to you about a servant you had in your employ."

Godfrey scowled, his eyes flashing.

"Is this a joke?" he demanded. "A servant? Who? Why?"

"Her name is Faith," Nicholas told him, knowing that his words were only incensing the man further. "And I must find her at once."

Godfrey's frown deepened.

"She up and vanished a week back. Good riddance to bad rubbish. I knew she was trouble when Edith brought her home. Found her sobbing outside a saloon somewhere of all places and gave her employment. My wife and her bleeding heart. She helps all the transients and I am made to suffer for it."

"What saloon? Where?"

"What is the meaning of this, Nicholas? You are beginning to make me question my decision in permitting a union between you and Chasity."

Suddenly, Nicholas could think of no worse fate than marrying his bore of a daughter. Chasity did not hold a candle to the vivacious and spirited woman who had forced her way into Nicholas' life.

"I must know where Mrs. Hovington found her, sir. It is a grave matter."

"The Ship Saloon." Edith Hovington stepped from the shadows and nodded softly. "It was the Ship Saloon, not one month ago. I feared for her which is why I brought her home."

"Edith, this does not concern you in the least."

Nicholas nodded at her gratefully and spun to leave but not before Godfrey yelled out for him again.

"You will be wise to leave the riffraff in the gutter where it belongs, Nicholas. You would not want your good name besmirched by associating yourself with a harlot!"

Fury coursed through Nicholas' veins but he held his composure, turning to stare at Godfrey with narrowed eyes.

"I would sooner align myself with a harlot than tie my family to you, Mr. Hovington. Good day."

His pulse was racing as he realized what he had said but Nicholas could not bring himself to regret it. His only concern was finding Faith and ensuring she was safe.

~ ~ ~

Nicholas found the Ship Saloon without incident but he understood why he was given such a leering look when he asked a local cowboy for directions.

It was not merely a saloon but a brothel also and the strait-laced Nicholas could not bring himself to enter the noisy tavern. The place was unlike any he had ever entered, the boisterous piano music emanating through the streets despite the early hour of the morning. Men spilled out, fighting loudly and Nicholas remained by Scout, unsure of what to do next.

She would not come to a place like this willingly, he thought, his dismay mounting in his gut. *If she is in there, she has been taken here by force.*

It was all the motivation he needed to push his way inside the saloon and make his way up to the barkeep.

The din was nearly unbearable as he approached the lanky bartender.

"What'll be, pardner?"

"I am seeking a girl," Nicholas explained and the man sneered.

"Well we got all kinds. What's yer pleasure? Blonde, dark?"

"Red haired," Nicholas heard himself say before he could think. The man nodded, his eyes lighting up.

"As it happens, I got me a nice redhead all ready for you upstairs," he told him. "Second door on the right side. Make sure ya pay her up front."

Nicholas shuddered and turned, hoping that the girl upstairs was not Faith but as he ascended, he knew he would find her there.

Gently, he rapped on the door but there was no answer.

Silently, he prayed to God to give him strength to endure whatever it was he might find beyond the closed door but even so, he was unprepared for what he saw when he entered.

Indeed, it was Faith, scantily clad in a black corset and ribbon tied about her fair neck but neither did a thing to hide the terrible bruises on her face.

Her back was to him as she stared out the window but her side profile told Nicholas everything he needed to know.

"What will it be?" she asked dully and Nicholas felt his stomach lurch in shock and sickness.

"Who has done this to you?" he demanded and Faith whipped her head around to look at him.

"Nicky!" she choked. "H-how did you find me?"

"That matters not," he told her firmly, his eyes scanning the room for more decent apparel. "You must dress and come with me at once."

She shook her mass of curls heavily, tears welling in her eyes.

"Donald will only find me again," she whispered. "There is no point. Every time I run, he brings me back again, him and his goons."

"This time he will not," Nicholas told her firmly. "Dress at once. I will meet you downstairs."

"Nicholas, you must not!" she protested. "They are dangerous men who will kill you for less than stealing away a source of income."

"You must leave this to me," he told her tautly. "Do as I instruct if you wish to leave this place."

He paused.

"You do wish to leave, do you not?" he asked and she sobbed.

"Of course! Why do you think I refused to leave your home? If Donald had not found me, I would still be there, insisting you marry me."

She closed her eyes.

"I am sorry for all I put you through. I know I had no cause to intercept that letter but I had seen you with Miss Chasity and I knew you intended to propose marriage to her. I thought it was my clearest route to safety, if I could only convince you to marry me instead."

"It was a harebrained scheme," Nicholas growled.

"I know," she sighed, opening her eyes. "Will you ever forgive me?"

"Perhaps at another moment. I have bigger matters to worry about now."

He opened the door and made his way back down into the tavern, his mind whirling frantically. He had only one plan in his head and if it failed, he did not know how else he would save Faith from a terrifying future in the brothel.

"Done so soon?" the barkeep leered.

"She will be leaving with me," Nicholas told her. "She belongs to me."

The barkeep snorted, apparently thinking that Nicholas jested.

"She belongs to the house," he replied curtly.

"No," Nicholas replied coldly. "She is my wife and I am bringing her home where she belongs."

"Your wife?" he whooped. Nicholas slowly became aware of the other men listening and a small group formed around him but he held his ground.

"She and I were married a week ago and if you insist on keeping her here, I will see that the Sheriff pay you a visit. Stealing a man's wife, particularly a wealthy man with good community standing is not a wise thing to do."

The barkeep, whom Nicholas was certain by now was the infamous Donald, glowered at him.

"You married a whore!" he spat furiously but Nicholas did not flinch.

"I will see my wife home now."

"If you are lying to me about this," Donald hissed. "I will reclaim her."

"If you come onto my property again," Nicholas replied evenly. "I will see you killed."

Donald seemed stunned by Nicholas' words and Faith appeared in saloon.

"Get the hell out of here!" Donald snarled. Nicholas extended his arm to show Faith from the tavern and the two hurried toward Scout who was tethered nearby.

They galloped away from the heart of Wyoming and Nicholas could feel Faith's heart hammering as fast as his. Neither spoke until the saloon was far from sight and it was Faith who broke the silence.

"Nicky, he is not fibbing. When he learns that we are not married, he will come back for me. He is not afraid of you or anyone else."

Nicholas was quiet for a long moment, thinking about his next words. In a week, this woman had altered his life in ways he could not have foreseen. Would he have ever considered a future with such a woman before the events of the past seven days? Likely not but suddenly idea of being with anyone else seemed insurmountable.

"Then he must never learn we are not married," Nicholas told her. Faith turned her head to stare at him, the horse trotting steadily back toward the Colville ranch.

"How will we keep it from him?" she whispered. "He is bound to learn the truth."

Nicholas shook his head and smiled gently at her.

"Not if we are truly to marry."

She gasped in surprise, her lovely green eyes huge.

"You need not marry me to keep me safe," she murmured. "Especially after all I have put you through."

"Then perhaps I will marry you because you have captured my heart," Nicholas replied softly.

AMISH COMPLICATIONS
MONICA MARKS

Her father cautiously steered the horse into the parking lot and Rachel gathered her things.

Her mother refused to look at her as she stepped from the cart, but she could see how white were her lips as they pursed together in anger.

"*Mammi*," Rachel said imploringly. "It is just a – "

"You do what you must, Rachel," Ruth interjected sternly, her green eyes still averted. "You are my daughter and I will love you regardless of what you choose."

Rachel swallowed the lump forming in her throat and glanced at her father desperately.

Daniel tried to smile weakly, but the expression seemed more of a grimace.

"Hurry along now, *liebchen*. You will be late," he told her, but Rachel knew it had less to do with her tardiness and more that he worried Ruth would fully speak her mind.

Rachel stifled a sigh and smoothed out her skirt, peering toward the building.

Perhaps they will go with someone else, she thought, the idea filling her with hope and disappointment simultaneously.

The problem was, Rachel didn't know what she wanted, not exactly.

Ever since Jacob and Lovina had announced their engagement two weeks earlier, Rachel had suddenly been lost in a void.

She felt like she was walking along in a never-ending dream, one which she would eventually wake and find that her best friend and secret love were not marrying in the coming year.

But it was no dream and Rachel knew she would never wake up.

As long as she remained in the district, Rachel was bound to live in the shadow of Jacob and Lovina's affections.

Rachel was also aware that the decision to interview for the teaching job at the elementary school in Holmesville was one which was breaking her parents' hearts, but Rachel was sure she could not spend one more minute in the district, knowing she would eventually see the newly betrothed couple anywhere and without warning.

This is your own doing, she reminded herself as she hurried toward the front of the school. *If you had made your feelings known, maybe Jacob would have chosen you. If you had said something, perhaps Lovina would not have fallen in love with him.*

It was a silly game of "what if" which she could not seem to stop playing with herself and Rachel had to separate herself from the heartbreak she was feeling.

But it was done and there was little she could do, not now. Even if things did not work out between Lovina and Jacob, he would be untouchable to her, Lovina's friend.

Rachel had missed her opportunity and it was gone forever.

Of course she had not explained her decision to her parents. They did not understand why she was preparing to leave the community when she had always expressed a desire to be baptized and embrace the *Ordnung.*

I am sure this will only be temporary, Rachel told herself as she entered the structure and walked into the office, presenting the most pleasing smile she could muster. *I will miss my home out here among the Englisch and go running home.*

Rachel also had to face the fact that she was assuming she got the job as a teaching assistant in the small school.

"May I help you?"

The receptionist peered at her through spectacles perched at the edge of a bird-like nose. Her lips seemed to form a slash as she studied the dark-haired woman in homespun clothes.

"I have an interview with Principal Cotton," Rachel explained. "My name is Rachel Littwiller."

"An interview for what?" the woman demanded, and Rachel noted the name on her plaque read "Amy Wheeler."

"A teaching assistant," Rachel replied quietly, her back tensing slightly at the open expression of disdain on Amy's face.

Do they not keep calendars with appointments? Can she not just look at the time slot?

Of course Rachel did not speak her questions aloud.

"*Teaching assistant?*" Amy echoed, arching a thin, painted eyebrow. "Really? Are you sure?"

Rachel did not know how to respond to the woman's open skepticism but before she could say a word, the door to the inner office opened and a robust man in his fifties exited.

"Ah! You must be Ms. Littwiller! Please, come in. You're right on time."

Rachel exhaled slowly, grateful that Principal Cotton seemed more amiable than his sour-faced receptionist.

"Good luck," Amy said snidely, a snicker in her voice and Rachel's brow creased.

Why is she being so hostile toward me? She does not know the first thing about me.

She did not have time to pursue the concern as Principal Cotton ushered her into the room and gestured for her to sit down.

"I am so happy to meet you, Rachel. Bishop Miller and I have been friends for many years and he speaks so highly of you. Although I must say this is the first time he has ever recommended anyone in the district for a teaching position."

Rachel peered at him with vivid green eyes, searching for the right words.

"He is a good man, Bishop Miller," she finally offered. "And I appreciate you taking the time to meet with me."

Principal Cotton nodded in agreement.

"That is why I trust him wholeheartedly when he suggested you. We are thrilled to have you onboard at Thomas Jefferson Elementary."

She gazed at him, shocked.

Is he hiring me without so much as an interview? Based on Bishop Miller's word?

"You have already made your decision then?" she breathed, a combination of happiness and dread sweeping over her.

"Unless you have anything you would like to discuss before we sign the paperwork," he replied, smiling broadly. He opened a manila folder and began shuffling through a pile of papers.

Rachel shook her head, stunned at what she was seeing.

The papers are simply ready to be signed! I got the job!

"No!" she cried. "Thank you very much! I will not disappoint you!"

Principal Cotton chuckled.

"That is the last thing I worried about," he assured her, extending his hand. "You will start on Monday. Classes commence at eight a.m., but you may wish to be here early, so you are able to discuss your duties with Mrs. Verhoot. That is whose class you will be assisting. Have you any questions at all for me, Rachel?"

She gulped, thousands of words flooding her mind, but she could not formulate a proper question.

Instead, she shook her long black braid and accepted his outstretched palm.

"Thank you!" she said again, realizing she had already thanked him profusely but she could not think of anything else to say.

Principal Cotton beamed.

"You have earned it," he said jovially, pushing the pages toward her to sign. The next few minutes consisted of Rachel writing her signature, but she was too overwhelmed to notice what she was signing.

It was not until Rachel was back at the wagon where her parents waited did she wonder what it was she had done to deserve the job.

Surely there are others more qualified than me, she thought. *Ones with more education or experience...*

"What did he say?" Daniel asked as they started back toward the district.

He was the first one to break the silence in the wagon, Rachel lost in thought over what had happened and how fast it had occurred.

Rachel's excitement was fleeting as she realized she had to break the news to her parents.

"I have the job," she murmured, trying to keep the glee from her voice.

Ruth stifled a sob, but Daniel gave her a rueful smile.

"I had no doubt you would get it," he told her. "They are fortunate to have you. The children in the district adore you."

Rachel eyed him gratefully, but the rest of the trip home was made in silence as each family member was consumed with their own thoughts.

Rachel was already wondering if she had made a mistake but as Daniel guided the cart back toward their house, she noticed a couple walking up the road.

As they drew closer, Rachel's heart froze in her chest.

It was Lovina and Jacob, their heads close as they seemed lost in conversation.

At the last minute, they turned in unison, seeming surprised by the sound of hooves.

"Rachel!" Lovina cried, waving.

Daniel slowed the cart and Rachel forced a smile onto her face.

"*Moin*," she greeted the couple, willing tears not to well in her eyes.

"Come with us for a walk," Lovina implored. "We are headed to the lake."

"I can't," Rachel responded, a sudden resolve growing inside her. "I must pack."

Lovina stared at her uncomprehendingly.

"Pack?" she echoed, glancing at Jacob who seemed equally confused and Rachel nodded.

"Yes," Rachel said firmly. "I am leaving for Holmesville this weekend."

And as she said it, studying her best friend's face register shock, Rachel suddenly was sure she was doing the right thing.

If I am made to stay here and see their happiness while my heart breaks, I will go mad.

"Okay boys and girls, settle down," Mrs. Verhoot instructed, clapping her hands together. "We have a new teacher today."

The unruly mass of children blatantly ignored the older woman and continued to yell and squabble amongst themselves.

Mrs. Verhoot tried again.

"Children!" she called, thumping her coffee mug against the table. "Attention please!"

A few eyes trained toward the front and suddenly one girl tittered as she saw Rachel. She pointed and whispered to her friend who turned to spread the secret to the next group.

Soon, the class was silent but for a sprinkling of giggles as the children stared at her.

"Take your seats, children," Mrs. Verhoot instructed, seeming relieved that they were finally listening. "Everyone, this is Miss Littwiller."

The quiet sniggering became blatant laughter.

Rachel turned to her co-worker in confusion.

"Quiet down now!" Mrs. Verhoot growled. "Miss Littwiller – "

The chortles grew louder, and Rachel's eyebrows knit in confusion.

"Why are the chuckling?" she asked Mrs. Verhoot, not understanding the joke but the older woman did not answer, scowling at the class.

"That is enough!" she cried, her face growing red. "Miss Littwiller is your elder and commands your respect. She is here to help with your studies. Am I understood."

They tried to contain themselves, but the smirks did not disappear from their collective faces and Rachel could feel her ears growing red with humiliation.

She knew they were laughing at her, but she could not say why.

As the day progressed, she heard them tittering about her name and her clothes and as lunchtime came, Rachel was sure she was crimson with embarrassment.

She gathered her lunch from the staff room and looked around for a place to eat in peace.

There were several tables already occupied by staff, but no one offered her a place at theirs and Rachel was too shy to ask for a seat.

In fact, the other teachers seemed determined to avoid eye contact with Rachel, deliberately turning their shoulders away from her as if to discourage her from approaching.

You are imagining things, she told herself. *Those children have made you irrational.*

Still, Rachel did not take the chance that they would reject her.

Instead, she took her bag and wandered out of the room toward the playing field in search of sanctuary.

Her long skirt swirled around her ankles and she finally found a quiet spot near the edge of the property beneath a giant oak.

Tucking her legs beneath her, Rachel flipped her long braid over her shoulder and reached inside the lunch bag for some bread and cheese.

She had not had much of an opportunity to do shopping since moving into her small apartment on Taylor Street, but she had not realized how hungry she would find herself by lunchtime.

Tomorrow I will pack a heftier lunch, she told herself. *Who would have thought that this job would be so tiring?*

Rachel tried not to think about the impending hours.

"Are you Miss Littwiller?"

She gazed up at the speaker, a tall, thin man in his early thirties in a Polo shirt and loose-fitting jeans.

He was handsome in an academic way, wire rim glasses hiding long lashed blue eyes.

"Yes," she replied.

He presented her with a quick smile and even in its fleetingness, Rachel noticed how white were his teeth.

"Principal Cotton is looking for you," he said. "They made an announcement in the school on the public announcement system, but I suppose you didn't hear it all the way out here."

Rachel rose, shaking her head so her prayer cap strings slapped her mouth gently.

"Thank you," she said, gathering her scraps of food and packing them back in the bag.

He watched her with curious eyes and Rachel felt a slow blush creep up her neck.

"Is there something else?" she asked, and he seemed surprised to find he was still staring at her.

Quickly he shook his head.

"Uh...no...I'm David Mathers, by the way."

She didn't respond, hurrying back toward the school and through the corridors.

That was very rude of you, Rachel reproached herself. *He is the only person who has reached out to you since you've been here, and you did not even introduce yourself properly.*

Rachel knew it had nothing to do with the kind stranger and more to do with her nerves. She wondered what Principal Cotton wanted with her now.

Have I done something already? I have only been here for four hours!

It seemed suddenly as if everyone was staring at her whereas earlier, she could not catch one person's attention.

Inside the office, Amy leered at her from the desk, causing Rachel's anxiety to mount.

"Go right in, Rachel," she instructed in a smug tone. "Principal Cotton is waiting for you although he did call for you ten minutes ago."

Rachel did as she was told, rapping on the inner door gently.

"I said go in!" Amy snapped. "Can't you follow simple instructions?"

Again, Rachel ignored the receptionist and waited for Principal Cotton to acknowledge her.

"Come in, Rachel," he called, and she noticed that his tone was much less friendly than it had been the first time they had met.

"You wanted to see me, Principal Cotton?" she asked tentatively as she entered.

He glanced up from his computer screen, his jaw tightening slightly as he saw her.

A chubby hand waved her further inside.

"Please sit down. I feel like we had a miscommunication when I hired you," he started. "But there are some things we need to discuss immediately, some concerns I have."

Rachel felt her back grow rigid and she chewed on her lower lip.

I have done something wrong!

"Such as?" she choked, wracking her brain to think of what it was.

Principal Cotton cleared his throat and shifted his eyes downward.

"For example, your attire. Now I realize that you come from a simple lifestyle, but the parents of the students expect a certain decorum from the teachers. We cannot have you dressed so..."

He trailed off and Rachel tried not to gape.

Principal Cotton cleared his throat and seemed to balk at Rachel's open-mouthed stare.

"You understand I mean no offense, Rachel," he told her. "I am only explaining to you the requirements of the job."

"I see," she mumbled. "Anything else?"

His porcine eyes darted around the room again before resting on her face.

"Perhaps we should shorten your name to Miss L. It will be easier and less distracting for the children to absorb."

Suddenly, it made sense; the whispers and mocking.

I am expected to appease the children when they are acting cruelly? What kind of adults will they grow up to be if not taught to respect their elders? She wondered.

Rachel's stomach seemed to flip as she gazed at her boss, unsure of how to react.

One part of her wanted to run from the office and forget she had ever decided to take such a wretched position but when she thought of Jacob and Lovina walking arm in arm near her home, there was only one option.

"Rachel, please don't look so devastated," Principal Cotton pleaded. "These changes are as much for your benefit as they are everyone else's. If you give these parents and kids things to take issue with, they will come at you mercilessly. I am only trying to make the transition easier for you."

Rachel swallowed thickly and nodded.

"I understand," she whispered, casting her eyes toward her hands. "I will ensure I am better dressed tomorrow."

The principal cleared his throat and shook his head.

"I was thinking you could go shopping now," he told her. "Take the afternoon to do that and start fresh again tomorrow. We'll pretend today never happened."

As if it would be so simple to forget about today, Rachel thought miserably.

There was no room for argument in his tone and she bobbed her head stiffly.

"As you wish," she replied quietly, rising from the edge of the chair.

They did not exchange another word as Rachel left the office, avoiding Amy's smirk. As she ventured out of the office, she heard the mean-spirited woman speak loudly.

The conversation was meant to be between herself and Principal Cotton, but Rachel could tell Amy wanted her to hear.

"That's what you get for hiring a child with Grade Eight education!" Amy snickered. "What were you thinking, Charles?"

Rachel paused to hear the older man's response.

"What choice did I have, Amy? It's not like we are teeming with applicants out here in Holmesville. She will do – for now. It's in her contract. We can replace her on a whim if someone better comes along."

Shock filled Rachel's body and she ran from the school, her hands trembling.

She had disappointed her parents, uprooted her life in the district and walked into something far worse.

Or was it?

Once more, the image of Lovina and Jacob's wedding filled her mind and Rachel was sure that nothing would be more torturous than returning home to see that.

You must give this life a chance, she tried to reassure herself. *As Principal Cotton said, this is an adjustment for everyone. I cannot make an informed decision after one day.*

Yet as she made her way into the center of town, searching for a decent place to buy Englisch clothes, Rachel wondered if she would ever belong anywhere ever again.

The following day, Rachel was at school before anyone else.

She nodded at the janitor as she made her way into Mrs. Verhoot's classroom, determined to have a better day.

The previous night, she had stayed awake, thinking of ways to win over her co-workers and the children.

She was feeling confident when she finally fell asleep at three o'clock in the morning but in the light of day, she was no longer certain she knew what she was doing.

You will be a wonderful teacher, she promised herself. *No matter what Principal Cotton and Amy think of your. You will make yourself indispensable to the school and they will not even consider another for your position.*

As she sat at the desk, writing down her ideas for Mrs. Verhoot, she suddenly got the sense that she was being watched.

Rachel's head bolted up and she gasped slightly as she recognized the man in the doorway.

"Uh, hey," he said. "Sorry, you just looked so lost in thought there and I didn't want to interrupt you."

She simply stared at him in confusion.

His brown eyebrows made a vee and he walked toward her.

"I'm David Mathers. I teach Fourth Grade – we met yesterday on the field," he explained, and she nodded quickly.

"Yes, of course," she replied. "Rachel Littwiller. I...I'm sorry if I was rude yesterday."

He shook his head.

"I understand you're having a classic Thomas Jefferson start here," he replied dryly. "Don't apologize to me. I'm sorry this place is so wretched to newcomers."

He offered his hand and she accepted it briefly before darting her eyes back toward the page before her.

"You look much different out of your dress," David said and his face blushed scarlet. "I mean, you look different wearing slacks."

Rachel swallowed a smile, shaking her head.

It felt odd not wearing her prayer cap, but she did not know if it was permitted and she didn't want to be called back into Principal Cotton's office.

"I did not realize there was a dress requirement before I started," Rachel explained, her face turning pink at the memory of being called to the office.

David seemed annoyed.

"There are several things about this school which are unfair and unnecessary," he replied curtly, and Rachel glanced up at him in surprise. There was a slight anger in his voice but before she could ask him anything further, Mrs. Verhoot appeared at the doorway.

"Oh! Don't you look nice, dear!" the woman cried, clapping her hands together in her regular dramatic fashion. "Doesn't she look nice, Mr. Mathers?"

David shrugged and turned to leave.

"I think she looks uncomfortable being forced to wear something she doesn't want to wear," he replied but he was gone before anyone could respond.

Rachel felt a spark of hope in her heart as he left.

He was the first person she had met outside the district who didn't seem to dislike her.

Perhaps there was hope for her in the Englisch world after all.

The small feeling of victory did not last however, and by day's end, Rachel's nerves were frazzled.

The children seemed determined to make her life unmanageable, misbehaving, throwing things and getting into trouble.

Mrs. Verhoot had dismissed her recommendations, making Rachel feel like an incompetent fool as she condescendingly explained why her ideas would not work.

At lunch she still could not find anyone with whom to speak and she found herself looking for David, but he was not in the staffroom.

She considered asking someone where to find him, but she worried how that would be perceived when she was already under such fine scrutiny.

She did not see the Fourth-Grade teacher for the rest of the day and when Rachel finally found herself at the low-rise apartment building, she was looking forward to a bath and reading a book.

What she had not expected was seeing her mother waiting for her in the lobby, seeming out of place and uncomfortable.

"*Mammi!*" Rachel cried, hurrying to embrace her mother. "What are you doing here? Is it *Daed*? Leah?"

Ruth shook her graying head, eyeing her daughter's outfit. Rachel could see she was desperately trying not to pass judgement with her eyes.

"No, liebchen. Everyone is fine," Ruth replied. "I have come to see your apartment."

Rachel gave her a sidelong look.

"All right," she said slowly and leading the way to her ground floor unit. "Are you certain everyone is well?"

Ruth nodded quickly, and Rachel sighed in relief.

She is worried about me, she realized. *A mother always knows when her child needs her.*

"Would you like some tea, *Mammi*?" Rachel asked as they entered the small apartment.

"No, Rachel, I would like for you to come home now."

The words were not surprising, but they caught Rachel off guard nonetheless.

She exhaled heavily and faced her mother.

"Mammi, I cannot simply leave the job I just started," she told Ruth. "I have a contract, an obligation."

"You have an obligation to your community too, Rachel," her mother reminded her, and the younger woman cringed.

"*Mammi,* please, you must understand – "

"No, I do not understand but if this is truly what you want, I cannot stop you and I will always love you. That said..."

Ruth trailed off and grasped Rachel's hands.

"Gideon Smith has been asking about you since you left. He was gravely disappointed to hear you had taken this job."

Rachel cocked her head to the side and studied her mother's face.

"Really?" she asked.

Rachel was not sure what to do with that information.

Gideon was an older man, widowed with a young daughter whom Rachel cared for a great deal. But to consider Gideon a suitor? Never. Rachel's dreams had always included Jacob.

But now Jacob is spoken for. And you are alone in a world where you are disrespected and demeaned. Gideon Smith would make a decent husband.

"Perhaps you should consider your options for marriage, Rachel," Ruth said softly. "I see you are thinking about it."

Rachel knew she would never feel toward Gideon as she did Jacob.

But it was still the prospect of marriage.

You vowed to give this job a chance, she reminded herself. *You have not even given it two full days. And what kind of marriage would it be to Gideon? A marriage to a man you do not love while you see the one you do with someone else.*

Rachel shook her head.

"No, *Mammi*," she said firmly. "I must complete my contract with the school. Perhaps later I can think about coming home."

Ruth's mouth became a fine line of anger, but she did not argue.

"Your father warned me not to come. He thought that you would say such a thing, but I wanted you to know that you are not forgotten in the district."

Rachel nodded slowly.

"*Danke, Mammi*," she said earnestly. "I needed to hear that."

Mother and daughter locked gazes and Ruth touched her cheek gently.

"Everything will work out the way *Gotte* intends, *liebchen,*" Ruth told her. "You must trust in His will."

Rachel hoped her mother was right.

As the second progressed, Rachel found herself thinking of Gideon Smith more often.

She asked herself if she was being unreasonable by dismissing him so easily.

After all, she did adore his daughter, Ivy and he was a kind man from the little she knew of him. It was slightly startling to learn that he had affections for her.

I imagine that Jacob would be stunned to learn I had feelings for him also, she mused and in the end, it always circled back to Lovina and Jacob.

By Friday afternoon, Rachel decided she would return to the district and visit her family.

She missed her parents and sister terribly, but she was plagued by the fear of seeing her best friend with Jacob.

Surely it must get easier, Rachel thought as she packed up her attaché case and looked around to ensure she had not forgotten anything.

A quiet knock on the door caught her attention and she turned to see David Mathers in the doorway.

"You made it through your first two weeks," he told her, grinning. "And you are still standing!"

She smiled and nodded.

"I suppose that is something to be grateful for," she agreed.

"How are the kids treating you?" David asked, and Rachel peered at him for a long moment without speaking.

Slowly, his beam faded.

"Uh oh," he commented. "That badly?"

Rachel shook her head.

"No," she answered as if suddenly realizing that the children had not been as mischievous the past day or so. "They have been quite good, in fact."

David's face brightened.

"Well that's good," he remarked. "I knew it would just be a matter of time before you found your groove. What about the staff?"

Rachel laughed.

"Well you have been very kind to me, but I believe everyone else thinks I have no right to be here."

David frowned.

"It doesn't matter what anyone else thinks," he growled in annoyance. "You are doing a wonderful job reaching the children. I wish the adults would act with some maturity too."

Rachel was slightly taken aback by his outburst.

"You do not think highly of the teachers?"

David shrugged, trying to appear nonchalant but Rachel could read the irritation in his eyes.

"It is not that they are bad teachers, but they act like small children themselves. They have their own tables in the breakroom and gossip about one another. It is just like being in high school," he grumbled. "I think it has much to do with the small-town mentality. In city schools, the teachers are not so childish."

Rachel's eyebrows shot up.

"You have taught in city schools?"

"I used to teach in Columbus before I got transferred here. I have put out my resume to get in a school in Akron but who knows if a position will come available."

An unexpected pang shot through Rachel.

You can't leave me here! I have no other friends if you go! She wanted to yell but she held her reaction and smiled weakly.

"Well I am certain that you will do very well no matter where you go," she told him. He returned her beam and a short pause fell between them.

"So...uh, do you have plans for the weekend, Rachel?" he asked.

"I am going home to visit my family," she told him. "There is no service on Sunday this week, so I will have an extra day with my parents and sister."

David nodded.

"That sounds good."

They gazed at one another somewhat awkwardly and Rachel gestured at her bag.

"I should be going," she said. "I will see you Monday."

David nodded.

"If I haven't moved to Akron," he joked but the words sent another shiver of panic through Rachel.

What if he really does go to Akron? She wondered as she left the school.

She didn't want to think about it.

"You have come home!" Ruth gasped as Rachel walked inside the house.

"Just for a visit, *Mammi*," Rachel replied quickly, careful not to raise her mother's hopes unrealistically.

"We are happy to have you, *liebchen* but you should have told us you were coming," Daniel chided. "We people coming for supper tonight and you will be riddled with questions."

Rachel grimaced at the thought.

All week she had been at the mercy of strangers. The last thing she wanted was to endure the same treatment with those she loved.

"I should not have come," Rachel sighed, turning back toward the door.

"Do not be foolish!" Leah called, racing down the stairs. "We will be amongst friends tonight. *Daed*, you should not have made her feel shamed for returning home."

Ruth and Leah glared at Daniel and he looked at Rachel with contrition.

"Of course she should not feel shamed," he exclaimed. "You are always welcome home, *Lieb*. Come out of the doorway now and put your bag in your bedroom."

Rachel felt torn, glancing helplessly at her sister who ushered her onto the second floor.

"How is it living among the Englisch?" Leah demanded. "Tell me about your apartment!"

Rachel glanced at her sixteen-year-old sister who had not yet experienced Rumspringa and she tried to remember if she had ever been so fascinated with Englisch culture.

I never wanted to leave the community, Rachel thought and even when Lovina and the others were wearing Englisch clothes or smoking cigarettes, Rachel had known her place was in the district.

Yet at that moment, Rachel wanted to retreat back to her apartment in Holmesville.

The conflict inside her was real and while she was happy to see her family, Rachel could not stop comparing the luxuries she had inside her one-bedroom unit to the simple ways of the farmhouse.

"Rachel? Are you all right?" Leah asked, and the older sister forced a smile.

"Yes. You must come and visit me," she said, shifting her thoughts away from her new life.

"Will you come home and marry Gideon Smith?" Leah asked, and Rachel's green eyes widened in shock.

"Did *Mammi* tell you that?" she demanded. Leah nodded.

"I said no such thing," Rachel muttered. "No, I will not marry Gideon Smith."

"Who will you marry then?"

Rachel stared at her for a long moment.

"Maybe an Englischer," she replied haughtily, and Leah gasped.

"You are not coming back, Rachel?" she demanded. "But *Mammi* said – "

"What *Mammi* hopes and what is real are two different things," Rachel interrupted. "I have a job now at the school and perhaps it could be a career for me."

"You like it so much?" Leah asked, and Rachel cringed inwardly.

I cannot lie to her.

"Leah! Rachel! Our guests have arrived!" Ruth called from the downstairs landing.

"Come along," Rachel said, and Leah grabbed her arm.

"You cannot go like that," she breathed.

Rachel gazed down at her pantsuit and sighed.

She had forgotten what she was wearing.

"I will change and be down in a moment," she said.

As Leah left the room, Rachel peered down at her outfit once more.

She couldn't recall the moment when the clothes had become comfortable. It seemed that one day she had felt terribly uncomfortable in such foreign garments and the next they had become second skin.

Slowly, she put on a homemade brown dress and brushed her tresses away from her face.

As she peered at herself in the mirror, another obscure thought popped into her head.

I should see about acquiring a haircut.

"Rachel!"

"Coming *Mamm*!" she called back, whirling away from the mirror. She hurried down the stairs toward the sitting room where she froze in her tracks.

"Rachel! You have come home!" Lovina squealed happily, hurrying to embrace her. "Why didn't you tell us you were coming?"

She disentangled herself from Lovina arms and smiled at her friend's parents.

"I wanted it to be a surprise."

Jacob also grinned from the corner where he sat with his brothers and father.

"*Moin*, Rachel!" he called disarmingly.

Rachel stared at him, her mind beginning to turn.

For the first time since they had announced their engagement, she did not feel an overwhelming sense of heartbreak.

A small twinge affected her heartbeat, but it was nothing compared to the agony she had felt before.

"*Moin,* Jacob," she replied easily, and the words did not stick in her throat.

It is getting better! Rachel thought, a deep breath of relief passing through her.

As they gathered around to dinner, Rachel wondered what had changed.

She no longer found herself pining after Jacob or envying Lovina. Instead her mind was somewhere else, in a classroom, picking up her books at the end of the day.

She was not playing the "what if" game but glancing over at the threshold where David Mathers was waiting for her.

Nothing has changed except for me, she realized. *I am moving onward with my life.*

A sudden elation filled Rachel and she knew then what she had to do.

"Good morning, David," she called, and he started as he flicked on the light of his classroom.

"Rachel!" he gasped. "You surprised me. Why are you sitting in the dark?"

"It isn't dark," she laughed. "And I am Amish. I am used to much less lighting than this."

David chuckled and dropped his books on the desk in front of her.

"Did you have a good weekend?" he asked, and she nodded.

"I did. And you?"

David shrugged.

"It was not very eventful, but my weekends never are," he replied. "What are you doing here?"

"I came to ask you something," Rachel answered, slipping off his chair.

"Ask away."

"I wanted to know if you would eat lunch with me today."

His eyebrows shot up in shock.

"Really?" he laughed. "Are you asking me to your table?"

Rachel nodded.

"I thought we could start our own table. There is no need for us to be isolated while the others sit together."

His face lit up completely.

"I would like that," he replied.

Rachel steadied her trembling hands and nodded.

"Are you okay, Rachel?" David asked gently, and she bobbed her head enthusiastically.

"I think so," she told him, and she meant it.

She didn't know where things would go with David or if they would go anywhere at all, but Rachel did know that each day she spent among the Englisch taught her more about herself and that was not something she was going to give up on, especially not when she had an ally on her side.

While she loved her family and her community, Rachel was in no rush to return, not until she had fully experienced what she was just getting a taste of; her independence.

"Why are you staring at me like that?" David asked.

"Tell me more about Akron," she said.

"ABIGAIL'S DILEMMA"

Abigail Esh watched as the familiar hills and plains of her small Pennsylvania community fell into view. It had been a long buggy ride; they had been travelling for half a day.

She felt a small stab of excitement, at the thought of finally coming home. She had been staying with some friends of her family, who were English, for the past month. It was all part of her *rumspringa*. She had sampled many things in the big city, including going to art galleries and English restaurants. It had been enjoyable, of course, and she wouldn't change the experience for the world.

But she wanted to return to her community, and start life as a fully committed adult Amish. She was ready.

At last. Her family's farmhouse was in view.

As the buggy pulled up, her eyes took in every detail: the old ramshackle farmhouse, the outbuildings and hen house. Home.

The front door opened, and her mother was down the veranda steps. Her eyes were shining in excitement.

"Abigail! We thought you'd never get here," she remarked.

Abigail stepped down from the buggy, embracing her mother. It felt like she hadn't seen her in years.

"Mammi! It is so good to be home," she said. "Where is everybody?"

Mrs Esh smiled, a bit indulgently. "Daughter of mine, have you forgotten the routine already?" They walked up the steps to the house, arm in arm. "Your father and brothers are in the fields, of course. They will return for lunch, as is always the way. Your sisters are quilting, over at Mrs Troyer's, as they do every Tuesday."

Abigail flung herself onto the living room sofa as soon as they entered. "It was such a long trip, Mammi. I feel black and blue all over."

"How are the Carlisles?" Mrs Esh walked to the kitchen as she spoke, getting the coffee she had just made and two cups.

"Very good." Abigail sat up, rubbing her eyes. "They send their best wishes. It was a bit of a whirlwind, staying with them."

"I could imagine." Mrs Esh poured the coffee. "Come, have your coffee. It will revitalise you."

Abigail did as her mother requested, walking to the table.

Suddenly, she stopped. She could see the figure of a man at the front door – tall, dressed in the traditional Amish clothing. He had taken his hat off.

Who was he? She had never seen him before. And her eyes seemed to be unaccustomed to the Amish dress. She had been so used to seeing English clothes that it stood out to her. Well, she would get used to it, again, of course.

"Mammi." Abigail gestured toward the door. "Someone is here."

Mrs Esh rose, approaching the door. "Oh, it is only Nicholas! He is helping your father and brothers; he has been here about two weeks, from another county." She opened the door. "Nicholas! What can I do for you?"

The young man smiled shyly, looking from Mrs Esh to Abigail. "I am sorry to disturb you, Mrs Esh. Your husband sent me to tell you not to prepare lunch today, as we are planning to work through."

"Work through?" Mrs Esh frowned. "Stay for a moment, Nicholas. I will prepare something quickly for you all to eat, which you can take back with you. You can't all work from dawn to sundown without food in your bellies. Please, come in and sit down while I get something ready."

Nicholas hesitated, then walked through the door.

"Abigail," Mrs Esh said, "Could you please pour Nicholas a coffee, while I get the food ready."

"Of course, Mammi," said Abigail, glancing sideways at the handsome, shy young man. Who was he? Why was he working here?

"I'm Abigail," she said. "Please, sit down."

The young man did as he was told. Abigail poured him a coffee, then sat down beside him.

"How did you come to work with us?" she asked, taking a sip of her own drink.

"I was looking for some short term work," Nicholas replied, blushing slightly. "I am on my *rumspringa*, and wanted to experience life outside my community for a bit. My father knows yours, from many years ago, and got in contact." He paused, staring at her. "I'm sorry, but you are Abigail, who has been on your own *rumspringa*?"

"*Ja*," Abigail agreed. "I have only just returned, after staying with some English friends in the city."

"Did you have a good time?"

"I did," Abigail said. She looked at his hands gripping the coffee cup. Strong, and firm. "But I am happy to be home. The city life is not for me. The Lord has made that very clear."

"I am glad," he said, smiling at her. He had the bluest of eyes, the colour of the sky on a bright summer's day.

Mrs Esh came back in, carrying a paper bag filled with sandwiches. She handed it to Nicholas.

"Please, finish your coffee," she said, as he stood up.

"Thank you Mrs Esh, but I must return to work," he said. "And thank you for the food. I am sure we will all appreciate it."

He smiled at Abigail, ducking his head. Then he left.

Abigail stared after him, sipping her coffee thoughtfully.

What a handsome young man. And such polite manners.

It was good to be home, for a lot of reasons. And it seemed that there was one more good reason, although Abigail hadn't realised when she had walked through the door.

The day was full of surprises.

***

Now that she was home, it seemed like she had never left. It was funny, how life worked in that way.

She had already been home a week, and was back into the old routine. And the most exciting thing of all was that Nicholas, the shy young man who was helping her family with the harvest, had asked her out on a date.

She didn't know where they were going, as she excitedly got herself ready on Saturday night. But she knew that Nicholas would take her somewhere appropriate, as well as fun. They had just clicked, right from the moment that she had laid eyes on him at the front door.

But he was shy. She had found many reasons to go and disturb her family as they worked, sometimes bringing snacks or drinks. Her brothers would grin at her – they knew what she was up to. She didn't usually come to visit them so often. It had worked. Eventually, Nicholas had asked her out.

Now they sat in Stoll's restaurant in town, having just finished a hearty meal and laughing over a coffee.

Abigail had never been able to speak so easily to a boy. It was like they couldn't keep up with everything they wanted to say to each other. She felt a glow within her, as she looked at him.

They were just thinking of leaving when the door to the restaurant opened. Abigail turned to look automatically. Then wished she hadn't.

Oh, no. It was Christian Raber. She swivelled quickly in her seat, staring straight ahead. Her heart had started to thump uncomfortably. Maybe, if she was lucky, he hadn't seen her.

But her luck wasn't in. She heard his footsteps behind, approaching their table.

"Abigail." He wasn't smiling. "I didn't know that you were back in town."

She turned and looked at him, a bit fearfully. "Just a week," she said, quickly.

Nicholas was looking from Abigail to Christian. He seemed perplexed.

"I am Christian Raber," the man said, extending a hand toward Nicholas. "Abigail has lost her manners, it seems."

Nicholas took the man's hand, shaking it. He looked at Abigail. "And I am Nicholas Fisher."

She stood up, quickly. "We were just leaving, Christian," she said, walking toward the door. Nicholas' eyes widened, but he stood up, too, almost forgetting his hat on the table as he followed her. He had to go back to get it.

They exited, into the cold night.

Christian stood for a moment, staring after them.

His eyes were cold.

***

"What was that all about?" Nicholas had to run to catch up to Abigail.

She turned, stopping to catch her breath. "I'm sorry," she said. "I know that I appeared rude. But I didn't want to speak to him. He has this idea that he is in love with me, and I have given him no encouragement. Honestly." She blinked back tears, staring up at him.

"What does he do?" Nicholas was frowning, staring down at her.

"Oh, nothing much," said Abigail. She was appalled to find that her hands were shaking. Stop it, she told herself. "He is always polite. He just doesn't seem to understand that I am not interested."

She paused, shaking her head slightly. "I have told him enough times. But he doesn't seem to understand. When I next see him, at Church or Evening Sing or wherever, he asks me out again, as if he hasn't listened at all."

Nicholas assisted her up into the buggy. "I am sorry, Abigail. It is hard when someone doesn't listen to you."

"*Ja*," she agreed. She tried to shake the image of Christian, in the restaurant, out of her mind. She was on a date, with Nicholas. Handsome, caring Nicholas.

"Don't worry about it," she said. "I am sure he will realise, eventually."

They rode off, into the night.

They didn't look back. If they had, they might have seen the figure of Christian, standing in the dark street, staring after the buggy long after it had disappeared.

***

"He was in Stoll's Restaurant, Mamm."

Abigail was having a hot cocoa with her mother after the date. Nicholas had dropped her off half an hour ago.

Mrs Esh frowned. "Don't read anything into it, Abigail," she said. "It might have been just co-incidence. Who knows, maybe he needed to get something from Stoll's."

"At nine-thirty on a Saturday night?" Abigail was frowning, too. "No, I know him of old. He followed me there, I am sure of it."

"He never threatens you, does he?" Her mother looked at her over the brim of the mug.

"No." Abigail shook her head. "He is always polite. It's just a feeling I get. He always seems to be where I go, and he won't stop asking me to date him. I think after the first three negatives, he might get the message that I am simply not interested in him in that way. But he never does."

Mrs Esh stood up. "Time for bed, I think. I will talk to your father about this. We don't want to offend the Raber's, but Christian needs to know that he can't harass you. We will have to think it through carefully, though."

Abigail nodded, bringing her mug to the kitchen sink.

"I almost forgot." Her mother looked at her. "How was the date with Nicholas? We got so caught up talking about Christian."

Abigail smiled broadly. "It was lovely," she beamed. "I think that I really like him, Mamm. Do you think he likes me, too?"

Mrs Esh smiled, her eyes softening as she looked at her lovely daughter. "How could he not, my *lieb*?" she replied. "But I don't know how long he is staying for, Abigail. Your father said that he only needed help for a few weeks, and they are almost up. He lives in the next county."

"That's not so far," said Abigail. "We could write letters."

"So you could," agreed her mother. "But it really is time for bed now, Abigail. We have Church tomorrow, don't forget. And I have to be up very early to cook the goose for the lunch."

Abigail followed her mother up the stairs, preparing for bed. She glanced down at her Bible, thinking whether she should look at it tonight or not. It was very late. But she was still feeling jittery after her encounter with Christian, and felt like she needed some comfort.

Her head was drooping over the good book when she suddenly jolted fully awake. What had disturbed her?

She took her candle, and got out of the bed, walking to her window. She peered out into the darkness, but she could see nothing. She tried to shake the feeling of unease away from her. She was being silly. She should blow out the candle, and climb back into bed.

And yet she stayed, staring out the window. It was complete darkness; not even the moon was out tonight, and a thick blanket of clouds had covered up the stars.

She dropped the curtain, and climbed back into bed.

But the unease didn't leave her. Instead, it invaded her dreams...

She was running.

In motion, she suddenly stopped. She looked down at her feet, willing them to move. But it was like they were frozen in quicksand; the more she tried to dislodge them, the firmer they set. She twisted and turned, in a frantic bid to free herself.

He was coming. She knew he was right behind her.

Suddenly, the quicksand turned to ice. She attempted to run, again. But her feet were sliding over the ice. She stumbled, trying to regain her balance.

She heard a noise behind her, and turned quickly.

It was him. She couldn't see him in the shadows, but she knew.

The ice started cracking underneath her feet. She watched it zig-zag, broken veins across the white surface.

And then she was gone, underneath the ice, plunged into cold, cold water.

She stared up, and saw him looking down at her, coldly...

She sat up in bed, breathing heavily. She could feel sweat sliding down her neck.

This had to stop. She didn't know what Christian's intentions were, but he had to know how much he was scaring her. She didn't think that he would harm her, not really. But he was behaving oddly, and she couldn't deny anymore that it was starting to affect her.

She lay back down, drifting back to sleep. Think happy thoughts, she told herself.

The image of Nicholas filled her mind. His handsome face, concerned for her that night when she had told him about Christian. The way that he had helped her down from the buggy when they had arrived home, holding her hand tenderly so that she wouldn't slip. She had looked into his eyes, and seen kindness. His eyes shone with the purity of his soul.

Nicholas. Was she falling in love with him? But she hardly knew him. It had only been their first date, and they had chatted a handful of times before.

And soon he would leave. Return to his farm in the next county, away from her. His *rumspringa* over, just like hers was.

Would she see him again?

The image of Nicholas was the last thing that she remembered as sleep finally claimed her – this time for the whole night.

****

Abigail yawned, trying to stifle it with her hand discreetly.

It was the next day, and she was tired. It had been late before she had finally drifted off to sleep. She looked around at the familiar faces at the church service, but she hadn't seen him yet.

Nicholas. Her heart leapt as she said his name in her head, over and over.

Where could he be?

She tried to concentrate on the service, but her mind was drifting. Her mother had told her that Nicholas had attended their church service since he had been staying with them. And he himself had said that he would see her there. He had been looking forward to her mother's baked goose with apple and cider gravy for lunch, as well.

She surreptitiously scanned the congregation, again. But then she saw Christian Raber, staring at her from the back row. Shivers coursed through her; her skin crawled like it had been invaded by an army of ants.

She looked to the front, trying to concentrate on the service.

But her eyes, sickeningly, were drawn back to him.

He hadn't stopped staring. But now he added a small smile.

She refused to smile back. It would just encourage him. Silly, she chided herself. Even turning her head to look at him again he would perceive as encouragement.

He had always been an intense boy, ever since they had shared a seat in the one room classroom down the road. She could remember that he often would be alone, kicking a stone in the playground while groups around him played. And when he had friends, it would always be only one person, or two. Usually children who were a bit odd, like himself.

She had never been anything but polite to him, but she had drawn the line at friendship. She just couldn't stomach his intense stares. How he had perceived her politeness as anything other than that was beyond her. And yet he had. He had been asking her out for over six months now.

At first, she had been flattered, despite herself. But then it had got annoying. He simply wouldn't listen to her, when she said no. And then he started turning up everywhere that she went: a visit to the bakery, or when she was perusing stalls at the market. Anywhere.

It was one of the reasons she had gone so far away for *rumspringa*. Abigail wasn't much of a traveller, really. She probably would have stayed closer to home. But she had needed a break from his constant attention.

The service finally finished, and people started socialising. She went up to her mother.

"Where is Nicholas?" she whispered. "I haven't seen him today."

Mrs Esh looked at her. "I'm sorry, I forgot to tell you, Abigail," she said. "Nicholas received a note this morning, about something urgent. He needed to return home immediately. I'm not sure if he will be back, my *lieb*. He was due to finish work soon with us, anyway." She looked at her daughter. "Cheer up! You can still write to each other."

Abigail felt her heart sink. She shouldn't be so disappointed, of course. They had only had one date, and Nicholas had a life of his own, far away.

But she *was* disappointed. She couldn't deny it.

She was staring at the wall of the barn, lost in her own thoughts. She didn't see Christian approach until it was too late.

"Abigail." He bowed, slightly. His cold eyes were assessing her, as always. She often felt he looked at her like something strange he had just discovered on the sole of his shoe.

"Christian, I'm sorry, but now is not a good time," she said, quickly. Why was he always silent when he approached her? If she had some warning, she could have scurried away.

"I hear that the young man you went on a date with last night has left us," he continued, as if she hadn't spoken at all. "Very suddenly. Did you know that Frannie Glick knows him and his family? She was just telling me that he has a fiancée, back home."

Abigail gasped. She shook her head. "No, Christian, I am sure that you are mistaken," she replied. "Nicholas didn't mention anything to me about a fiancée. He is an honourable man."

"Is he?" Christian smiled, coldly. "How well do you really know him, Abigail?"

She frowned. She supposed it was true, to a degree. She had only known Nicholas a week, after all.

But she trusted her instincts. He was a good man, she knew it. He wouldn't have deliberately deceived her about having a fiancée.

"Well, I shall talk to him," she said, turning away. "I really must go, Christian. I have to help my mother with the lunch."

She walked away quickly, ducking amongst people. Hopefully he wouldn't follow her.

Was it true? He had said he had got the information from Frannie Glick. She looked around, but couldn't see her.

She frowned. Oh, well. Frannie would turn up, sooner or later. And then she would ask her, how she had come by this information that Nicholas had a fiancée.

As Christian claimed.

She felt the skin crawling on the back of her neck. She looked around, and, of course, he was staring at her. An upsurge of anger shot through her. Would he ever leave her alone?

***

"He did mention a girl he had been dating…" Mrs Esh frowned, squinting her eyes, trying to remember. "Or was it that they had dated in the past? I'm sorry, Abigail. I simply don't remember. But he never mentioned a fiancée, of that I am sure."

Abigail frowned, too. It wasn't the simple yes or no answer that she was wanting. This was very frustrating.

She didn't have a right to demand an answer of Nicholas. They had made no promises to each other; it had only been one date, after all. But she also felt that he did owe her an answer, because it simply wasn't done to be dating someone behind his fiancée's back, if he had one.

If it was true, she never would have agreed to go out with him. It was as simple as that.

Restless, Abigail stood up. "Do you need me for anything else, Mamm? If not, I might go to my room, study my bible for a while."

Mrs Esh looked at her. "Of course, Abigail," she said. "Just come down to help with supper, that's all I require."

Abigail left, bounding up the stairs.

Mrs Esh watched her go, shaking her head slightly.

Her daughter was in a state, and had been since Nicholas had left so suddenly the day before. Mrs Esh was worried about her. It was unlike Abigail. And what was this business with Christian Raber? Abigail hadn't mentioned it to her until after her date with Nicholas. If it was true, it wasn't good, and they should intervene on her behalf. But what if Abigail was just being fanciful? The Rabers were good friends of theirs. Mrs Esh didn't want to cause conflict without reason.

She frowned, pondering. No, they would do nothing, for now. If Abigail continued to be worried, well, they would do something then.

She sighed. It was hard, being young. Navigating your way into adulthood. She might mention some bible passages that Abigail should study, to try to ease her mind.

***

Abigail finished the letter, signing her name at the bottom thoughtfully.

She had been in two minds about whether to write to Nicholas, but she was so wound up she didn't know what else to do. Even if she didn't send the letter, it had felt good to get her thoughts and feelings out onto paper.

She read back over what she had written. She had tried to not be too intense, but still convey her wish to continue corresponding with him. She hadn't mentioned anything about him having a fiancée, except to implicitly imply that if he was seeing someone where he lived, she would stop communicating with him.

She put the letter in an envelope, and sealed it. She wasn't sure of his address; she would have to ask her mother if she knew it.

She left it on her desk, propped up against her lantern.

It was time to help her mother with supper.

***

Outside the farmhouse, Christian could see Abigail leave her desk. He saw the letter. He could guess who it was to. And he knew how to solve this, as well.

He often watched her. He had found a position, quite hidden. He would come over the back way to the house, through the fields, being careful to avoid her father and her brothers working.

He didn't think that he was doing anything wrong. He had, after all, explained to her that he wanted to take her out. It was his intention to make her his wife. She was hesitant, and had said no, but that didn't unduly concern him. His father had told him that girls sometimes said no when they meant yes. His own mother, apparently, had refused his father a few times before finally agreeing to date him.

She just needed a little bit of persuasion, that was all.

He frowned, thinking of when he had walked into the restaurant and seen her on a date. It simply would not do. No other man was allowed to date his Abigail.

It had been a stroke of luck that Nicholas Fisher's father had suddenly needed him back at home; as soon as he had heard that, he seized the opportunity. Frannie Glick was away on her *rumspringa*, and couldn't contradict his story about a fiancée. Frannie was a friend of his, anyway, and as soon as she was back he would contact her and persuade her to corroborate the story.

He smiled. It was all going to plan. He had to get rid of Nicholas once and for all, discredit him in Abigail's eyes. And then he would be there, to pick up the pieces.

She would finally see that he was the one for her.

***

The letter had been sent. Abigail waited for a response, but none came.

Inside, she fretted a little. It was all so strange. She had thought that she and Nicholas had a real connection. But he wasn't responding to her – did that mean that what Christian said was true? That Nicholas had a fiancée back home, and that she had been a diversion while he was away?

But as the days went by, and no letter came, Abigail had to admit it to herself. Nicholas didn't care.

Oh, well. She went about her chores as normal, and smiled and laughed when she was required to. She let no one see her sorrow. It would get better, in time. Of course, it would. They had only known each other a short time. It wasn't as if it was a deep wound.

She studied her bible. The classic passage from Ecclesiastes 3:4, about there being a time for sorrow as well as joy, comforted her. She knew that life couldn't be good, all the time. You could learn from sorrow, and had to accept that sometimes there was sorrow in life. As surely as the tides ebb and flow on the shore, sorrow and joy would come and go.

So Abigail kept telling herself, as the days drifted into weeks.

***

The women sat around the table, picking up their needles to commence their quilting bee.

Abigail picked up hers with a sigh. It had been three weeks, and she had not received a word from Nicholas. It was time to let it go, put it behind her. They had connected, but he had decided that it wasn't worth pursuing. Or, he did have a fiancée at home, and he had been merely dallying with her. Abigail preferred to think it was the former; she didn't want her last impression to be that he was a dishonourable man.

They heard another buggy pulling up outside the farmhouse. The women looked at each other.

"Are we expecting someone else?" Mrs Esh turned to the women.

Frannie Glick walked through the door, puffing slightly.

"Frannie!" Mrs Mueller put down her needle. "We weren't expecting you! Aren't you supposed to be on your *rumspringa?*"

"*Ja,*" answered Frannie, smiling at the group. "I returned yesterday, a few days early. Mammi told me that you were meeting today, and I wanted to catch up with you all."

Frannie took her seat, and started answering questions about her *rumspringa.* She had been staying with cousins in Ohio, and had a wonderful time.

Abigail glanced at her as she worked. She was waiting for the break, so she could ask her about Nicholas. It probably didn't matter, anymore. But she wanted to know.

At last, the women started getting up. One went to the kitchen, to prepare coffee and snacks. Frannie rose, and walked to the window.

"Frannie," Abigail said, walking up to her. "It is nice to have you back. I was just interested to know. Christian Raber was telling me that you know Nicholas Fisher and his family."

"Who?" Frannie looked at her, a puzzled expression on her face. "I don't know any Nicholas Fisher, Abigail. I think you must be mistaken."

"Are you sure?" Abigail frowned. "Christian told me that you knew the family, and that Nicholas had a fiancée back where he lives."

Frannie continued to look at her, bewildered. "I have no idea what you are talking about, Abigail. The only Nicholas I know is Nicholas King, who we went to school with."

"I'm sorry," Abigail said. "I must have misheard him. Thank you, anyway."

She turned around, and walked out of the house. She needed to be alone, for a moment. She needed to think.

She sat down on a seat on the porch, thinking deeply.

Frannie didn't know the Fishers. She had never heard of Nicholas. Which meant one thing: Christian had lied to her. About Frannie knowing them, but also about Nicholas having a fiancée.

She felt herself go cold. This was getting serious.

Christian had always been an annoyance. But now, he was actively interfering in her life.

She didn't know what to do. Just that it had to stop, once and for all. He had no right, and she was going to make sure that he knew it.

***

Abigail dressed carefully for the meeting.

She had spoken to Mrs Raber, asking her could she come over for a visit. There was something she needed to discuss with her and her husband, urgently. She also requested that Christian be there for the meeting.

She didn't tell her mother. She knew that she would be concerned about making waves with the Rabers. It was something she was concerned about, too. But she also knew that it couldn't continue. Christian had to be stopped. And the best way of ensuring that was to enlist his parents. Abigail knew Christian. He was obedient to his parents, and his father ruled him with an iron fist.

And it was something that she felt must do, by herself. She had to stand up for herself, once and for all.

Mrs Raber opened the door, and led her to the kitchen table. Coffee and cakes were there, waiting.

"Oh, you shouldn't have gone to so much trouble," Abigail said. She was sweating, a little, and her hands when she took the coffee cup were shaking. She wasn't looking forward to this.

Mr Raber was already there, looking at her expectantly. And then Christian came into the room.

He didn't look happy. But he sat down at the table. Obviously, his parents had insisted.

"So." Mrs Raber looked at Abigail, expectantly. "What did you need to see us about so urgently, Abigail?"

Abigail cleared her throat. She must be strong, but she was very nervous. It could backfire on her, and the Rabers might evict her from their home, saying that she was lying.

How should she proceed?

"Thank you for seeing me," she stated. "I know you are all busy people. I needed to see you about Christian."

Christian looked at her, his face like thunder. She almost balked, but doggedly continued.

"As you know, Christian and I have known each other a long time," she said. "Since school. I have always liked him as a friend, but lately, Christian has been wanting to court me."

Mr Raber smiled. "Nothing wrong with that."

"No," Abigail continued. "There isn't. But I have told Christian many times that I am not interested in him that way, and he continues to pester me. He doesn't listen to my wishes."

Mrs Raber looked at Christian, anxiously. "Is this true, Christian? Have you been pestering Abigail, when she has clearly said no?"

"She wants to go out with me," Christian blurted. "I know she does! She just needs persuading. Isn't that so, Daed? You always told me that women often don't know their own minds, and need a firm hand."

Mr Raber frowned. "That is not what I meant, Christian. Yes, sometimes a girl takes a bit of wooing. But if a young woman has clearly said no to you, repeatedly, then you must do the honourable thing and accept her decision."

"But...but..." Christian shook his head, colouring. "I know that she loves me, deep down!"

Abigail looked at him, coldly. "That is wrong, Christian," she said. "I don't love you, and never will. I have no desire to hurt you, but you must accept what I say. I don't want to court you. I like you just as a friend." That was a little white lie. She didn't like Christian, at all. But she didn't want to completely destroy his confidence in himself.

"Abigail, your wishes will be respected," said Mr Raber, glaring at his son. "I will make sure of it. Christian will not bother you anymore."

"Thank you," breathed Abigail. She turned to Christian.

"I wish you well, Christian," she said. "I hope that you find the woman that you will marry, one who loves you. But she is not me. I hope we can still be friends. Will you shake my hand?"

She offered her hand across the table to him. He looked at it as if he might refuse, then he grudgingly shook it. Mrs Raber looked relieved.

"I must go," said Abigail, rising. "Thank you all so much for letting me speak, and taking me seriously. It means the world to me."

"God speed, Abigail," Mrs Raber replied. Mr Raber smiled at her.

It was over. Christian would not bother her, again. She knew the Rabers, and that they demanded complete obedience. Christian would not dare to defy them, now that they knew. She would have preferred that he realised by himself, but that might never happen.

She had to protect her life. He had already interfered in her budding relationship with Nicholas. She didn't want him to interfere for a minute longer.

***

Abigail was feeding the hens when a shadow fell across her.

Fear gripped her. Oh, no. It wasn't Christian back – was it?

She looked around. Then gasped. It wasn't Christian who stood there, but another tall man.

It was Nicholas!

She stood up, slowly. She couldn't quite believe that he was here.

He smiled at her, a bit tentatively. "Abigail," he said. "Your mother said that you would be here."

"Here I am," she replied, then could have kicked herself. Couldn't she think of anything better to say?

"Do you want to go inside?" He asked. "I need to talk to you."

She nodded, leading the way out of the hen house.

They sat at the kitchen table, staring awkwardly at each other.

"I thought..."

"I'm sorry..."

They laughed, as they realised they had both spoken at the same time.

"You go," said Nicholas, looking at her as if he had never seen her before in his life. It made her glow.

"I thought that you didn't want to see me again," Abigail said, biting her lip.

"I thought the same," Nicholas replied. "When you didn't answer my letter."

"What letter?" Abigail frowned. "I never received a letter from you. I wrote *you* a letter, which you never replied to!"

Nicholas shook his head, frowning. "I don't understand. I never received a letter from you. But I did send one."

Abigail stared at him, perplexed. Then understanding started to dawn on her face.

"It must have been Christian," she said. "I didn't realise he was going to that level. He must have been monitoring our mail box. Mamm leaves letters we want to send in there for Daed to collect and send when he gets to town."

"Christian?" Nicholas frowned. "That man who has been pestering you?" He paled, and stood up. "This is going too far. I will go around to his house, this minute!"

"Nicholas, sit down," Abigail said. "It's alright. I have spoken to his parents. He won't be bothering me anymore."

"Are you sure?" Nicholas sat down, slowly. "Because if he ever tries again, he will have me to answer to!" Abigail could see a vein throbbing in his temple. He was angry.

"So you care about me?" She looked at him, shyly.

"I do," he replied. "So much so, Abigail, that I travelled here today to speak to you, even though I thought you didn't answer my letter." He paused, looking like he didn't know what to say further.

"I care for you, too, Nicholas," she said, shyly. "Can we begin again? Like before Christian started interfering in our lives. He told me you had a fiancée, back home."

"He what?" Nicholas looked gobsmacked. "That is an outright lie! I would never have asked you out on a date if I had a fiancée. You didn't believe it, did you?"

"I tried not to," Abigail answered. "But when you didn't reply to my letter, I thought the worst. It was Christian, all along."

"We can begin again," Nicholas said, looking at her earnestly. "If you are willing?" He reached for her hand, across the table. "And God willing, of course."

"Nothing would please me more," Abigail replied. She took his hand. Happiness swelled up within her.

Christian was out of their lives. Nicholas cared for her.

The time for joy was upon them.

END

The Painted Lake

ABBY BARKER

Emma hadn't missed a sunrise since she was old enough to help Mama with the laundry, with the exception of that day last winter when she woke up with a cold that kept her bedridden. To Emma, the sun peeking over grassy horizon signified the beginning of all things: life, journeys, and the potential that comes with each new day. Waking up after sunrise would be like turning down a message of encouragement from God, which Emma couldn't bear to waste, so she woke every day at the crack of dawn ready to face whatever challenges arose and accept all graces given to her. This was a schedule that she intended to keep for all time.

This morning, though, she almost missed it. The night before she spent tossing around in her bed, sometimes staring at the ceiling, sometimes the wall, but almost never the backs of her own eyelids. She was restless, but careful to move softly as not to wake up her pig-tailed younger sister, Abigail, who would not have to feel this nervousness for another handful of years, if she would even feel it then. If it was up to Emma, she would have been baptized years ago, but Mama insisted that she take some time to "test her faith." But she already knew her faith to be true; in her heart she knew it. That was enough for her, why wasn't it enough for Mama? This was the last thought she had before finally drifting off to sleep just before dawn.

It seemed as if no time had passed when Abigail gently nudged her sister awake just as the sun began its morning assent.

"Emma! Em!" she half-whispered, "It's today. You've got to get ready. You've got to go so you can hurry up and get back to tell me everything! What do you think Auntie Willa is like? You have to drive a car!"

Emma couldn't match her sister's excitement, but Abigail was right about one thing: The sooner she left, the sooner the month in the city she and Mama had agreed on would be over and she could come home.

"Abigail, please!" she snapped, "I hardly got any sleep and I have plenty of time to pack my bag." She wouldn't have to pack much. In her letters, Auntie Willa insisted they would go shopping the moment she got settled in.

"The clothing is part of the experience," wrote Auntie Willa, "you won't need your bonnet in the city!"

Emma frowned as she rolled away from her sister and turned her back on the dawn. She wanted to stay in bed forever, but she'd settle for five more minutes.

***

After completing her morning chores, Emma changed into a simple, but flattering white linen dress she thought was suitable for traveling. She looked at herself in the mirror as she brushed her long, sun-streaked hair, trying to untangle the knots on her head and in her stomach. A furrowed brow shaded her wide, hazel eyes and her dusty pink lips were downturned in a nervous frown. Each stroke of the brush brought her a little comfort, but not much. There was a lot to be nervous about. She had never met Auntie Willa and they had only spoken through letters. Mama, while she couldn't contact Auntie Willa herself, suggested that Emma reach out before she left on rumspringa. If she had to leave her home, Emma thought, she might as well try to stay with a family member while she's away. Even if that family member left on rumspringa herself 19 years ago and was the only one of her friends not to return home.

Since Emma wasn't yet an official member of the church, she was allowed to write to her excommunicated aunt, but she did so begrudgingly and only at her mother's expressed wishes. Emma could tell that Mama missed her sister, which helped assuage her reluctance to reach out. If Mama still cared for her, she couldn't be all bad. Even so, that first letter was tough for Emma to write. It read:

Dear Auntie Willa,

We've never met before but Mama says you're her sister, which makes you my aunt. She says you used to look just like her, but your hair was always wilder. I have many aunts and uncles here at home, but you're the only one who lives in the city. Mama said it would be a good idea to write you even though you're not with the church anymore because I'm eighteen and she wants me to see the English world before I'm baptized. If I had it my way, I'd already be baptized by now but Mama thinks it's important to face temptation, and deny it, before I make my decision. If I already know there's nothing that could tempt me more than the Will of God, why should I bother with rumspringa? You're probably not the right person to ask.

Your niece,

Emma Byler

Emma was surprised by how kind Auntie Willa seemed in her reply. She told Emma how excited she was to hear from her oldest niece and that she missed the family "something fierce." She also said that she agreed with Mama that seeing how the other half lives, especially if Emma was going to choose to stay with the church, was incredibly important. The way she said "if" put Emma on edge, but she couldn't help but like her aunt after reading the rest of the letter. Auntie Willa wrote enthusiastically and earnestly, offering up personal details about herself (she had an apartment in Chicago with a collie-mix named Charlie), and ended almost every other sentence with an exclamation point. Eventually, Auntie Willa asked Emma to come stay with her for a while.

Emma instinctively put the brush back on the vanity in front of her before remembering the open suitcase next to her. She picked the brush back up and packed it away. Auntie Willa was already on her way. She offered to drive down from Chicago to pick Emma up since no one in her family owned a car, and their horse and buggy wouldn't be able to make the journey to the city. In her letters, Auntie Willa kept referring to it as a "road trip" in an attempt to make the long ride sound more fun, but Emma had never been farther from home than the next town over and the idea of sitting in a car, another thing she had never done, for hours on end was daunting. Just as she zipped up her bag she heard the sound of Auntie Willa's car pulling up to the house. She sat on her bed with the bag in her lap for a few minutes before meeting her aunt in person for the first time.

When Emma finally walked into her family's kitchen, Auntie Willa was sitting at the table with a cup of water that Abigail brought her. She was wearing a bright red t-shirt tucked into a bright, floral-print skirt that brushed her ankles. Her curly, chestnut hair had apparently never lost it's wildness, but was clipped back in a twist that made it look like the strands were trying to escape. She and Emma had the same eyes, which were staring happily at her from across the room. Mama couldn't see any of this while she stood at the sink washing dishes and her back turned to Auntie Willa.

"Emma!" she yelled, jumping out of her chair and almost knocking over the water, "Emma, I'm so frickin' excited to finally see your pretty face!"

Mama bristled and Abigail stifled a laugh at Auntie Willa's objectionable language. Emma just stood stock-still as Auntie Willa rounded the kitchen table, arms outstretched like a bird taking flight, and encircled her in an enthusiastic hug.

"Emma, we're going to have so much fun. I mean, of course you're going to be doing some very valuable thinking and learning, too," she shot a careful glance at her sister, "but that doesn't mean it won't also be tons of fun!"

This made Mama briskly dry her hands on her apron, step away from the sink and pivot towards the hugging pair.

"Now you listen, Willa. Emma is staying with you because I think it's a necessary part of a young person's life to look the world straight in the eyes, knowing everything they need to know about their choice, and say 'My priorities lie with God.' It's not about fun. It's about free choice and true faithfulness. I know you clearly don't see it that way considering the path you've chosen, but Emma isn't like you, Willa. She's steadfast and faithful and knows exactly what she's doing."

Auntie Willa was taken aback, but her arm never left Emma's shoulders.

"Jodie, please. I took this decision just as seriously as you did. I just used me 'free choice' a different way is all. I'm sorry that meant things had to turn out the way they did, but it was my choice. Just like this will be Emma's. So if Emma wants to have fun, we're gonna have fun! And if she doesn't, well, what are the odds of that?"

She gave Emma a subtle wink and playful jab at her side, knocking her a little off balance. She regained her footing and spoke up the newly found courage that having her aunt's support provided.

"If it were up to me I wouldn't even be going. Mama, you asked me to do this, so I'm going to do it, but you can't ask me not to have fun. You have to trust me to do the right thing. I don't plan on doing anything in Chicago that I wouldn't do here."

Auntie Willa scoffed gently at this.

"Sweetie, I wouldn't say that. Even riding the elevator up to my apartment is going to be something you wouldn't do here, but I get what you're saying. You and your mother both can rest assured knowing that I would never make you do something you weren't up for. Cross my heart."

She made an "X" in the air over her chest with her right index finger, but Mama didn't look convinced with her arms crossed over her own chest.

"You have to trust me to do the right thing," Emma interjected through the tension.

"Sweetheart, of course I trust you." Mama walked over to her daughter and embraced her. "I know it doesn't seem like it at the moment, but I'm proud of you and grateful that you're doing this. God will guide you. As long as you follow your heart and His word you'll make it through."

She kissed Emma on the top of her head and reluctantly let her go.

"I love you Emma."

"I love you too, Mama. Don't worry about me. I'll make the most of it."

Emma then walked over to her sister and gave her a hug goodbye while she chattered away about clothes, boys, and Navy Pier. She tried to soak up as much of Abigail's excitement as she could before picking up her bag and walking out the door. Mama and Abigail followed them out to the car. When she saw the vehicle, Abigail let out an excited scream and ran over to it.

"It's red!" she yelled back at Mama and Emma, as if she thought they couldn't see it yet. Emma approached more cautiously. It seemed safe enough, by the looks of it, but she knew it could move ten times as fast as any buggy. She imagined the car being pulled along by two of her family's horses and allowed herself a small smile. Auntie Willa offered to help Emma with her bag just as she got close enough to run her fingers along the cool, smooth surface of the car. The trunk popped open on it's own and made Emma jump. Auntie Willa dangled the keys in front of Emma's surprised face.

"Cool, huh?" she said with a grin. Emma only smiled back and nodded. "Well, it's time to hit the road. If you forgot anything we can just pick it up when we get into the city. Bye, Abigail! Bye, Jodie! I'll try to get her back here in one piece!"

Auntie Willa opened the passenger side door for Emma and she slipped inside. She watched her aunt walk around the car to her own side and hop in, flashing Emma a faux-nervous smile. Emma watched her aunt pull the seatbelt around her body and clip it into the buckle.

She took the cue and, after a little bit of fumbling, was safely buckled in. Auntie Willa put the key in the ignition and the car started with a low roar.

"You ready, Em? No turning back now!"

Emma didn't know if she was ready, but she knew she had to be.

"Yes, Auntie Willa. Let's go."

"That's the spirit!" Auntie Willa replied joyously as she pressed a button next to her to open the front two windows. "Wave to your mom and sister. They're gonna miss you!"

Emma stuck her hand out the open window and looked back at her family standing outside. Abigail could barely contain herself as she fidgeted from foot to foot waving frantically. Mama was her opposite, standing tall and still, neither happy nor unhappy about seeing her oldest daughter drive away to Chicago. Emma pulled her hand back inside just as the car began to move. Her stomach lurched, but the feeling receded the farther they drove from home. Auntie Willa turned on the radio and started humming along. Emma kept her eyes locked on the road in front of them, watching her neighbor's homes fly by out of the corner of her eye. Auntie Willa's words echoed in her mind. *No turning back now!* She was tempted to turn around to see what her house looked like from this far away, but she took those words literally. There will be time to turn around later, she reminded herself, but this was the beginning of a new journey and she was determined to face it head on.

***

The view outside Emma's window slowly morphed from just ripened soy and cornfields to suburban neighborhoods filled with cookie cutter homes and chain grocery stores. She spent the first hour or so of the drive silently watching the world around her change and she felt herself changing, just a little bit, with it. From the safety of the car she was slowly immersed in this new world and allowed herself to become accustomed to it, but she didn't know what to expect when she stepped out.

Auntie Willa had been mostly silent up until now. She happily sang to herself and understood that Emma was the type to quietly take things in before wanting to talk about them, but Auntie Willa was not that type and after an hour of quiet she had about reached her breaking point.

"Are you getting excited? I remember sitting on the edge of my seat about to burst when I left home for the first time."

"I guess I'm...surprised? I thought it would be harder to leave than it was. I thought things would feel more alien, but after passing through all of these towns that look the same it's starting to feel familiar. Does that make sense?"

'Totally! I was blown away by the first Target I saw, but by the ninth or tenth it definitely lost its mystery. Don't you worry, though, Chicago is gonna knock your socks off. I've lived there for almost two decades now and it still takes my breath away when I'm driving toward that skyline. I'm definitely gonna take you to the planetarium. You won't get a better view of the city, or the universe, from anywhere else. I swear, it'll change your life."

She agreed to go on this trip to reassure herself and her family that she wanted her life to stay the same. She hadn't given any thought to how she might come home changed. This thought both scared and excited Emma. For the first time, she allowed herself to think of the experience not just as a trial, but also as an adventure.

"I think I'd like that. Back at home the sky is filled with millions of stars at night. After dinner Abigail and I sometimes go out into the yard and lie down to look up at them. I know that most of them already have names, but we'd lie there and come up with names of our own. I usually picked names of people from the Bible. It's comforting to think God's people are looking down on us, but Abigail always named the stars after boys she likes," Emma giggled at the memory and Auntie Willa followed suit.

"You won't see many stars in Chicago. The sky's mostly filled with planes and helicopters, but you'll be able to see all sorts of things at the planetarium. All the stars named after your sister's crushes and then some!"

Emma tried to imagine how they got all the stars to fit inside one building when the entire skyline of Chicago rose up out of the rode in front of her. She'd never seen it before but she knew it couldn't be anything else. Auntie Willa glanced over at Emma and saw her eyes grow wide.

"Awesome, isn't it? Just you wait."

This feeling was not what Emma expected. She wanted to know what it felt like to be amongst those buildings, and all the people who live in them. She wanted to know how it felt to be a part of something so massive and seemingly intangible. The buildings look small on the horizon, but Emma was still struck by their size. She was so caught up imagining how it would feel to sit on top of the tallest building in Chicago and see the landscape change backward from city, to suburb, to home that she almost forgot she'd planned to go back.

***

Auntie Willa had prepped her for the elevator, but she still gripped the railing with white knuckles when it began its assent. Auntie Willa lived on the nineteenth floor of a high-rise with two bedrooms and a sweeping view of Lake Michigan. One bedroom was Auntie Willa's and Charlie had unofficially occupied the other until the day before. He was a little put out when Auntie Willa dragged his bed and toys out into the living room, but immediately changed his tune when he met Emma. She didn't even have a chance to realize that she'd never been this high up before Charlie bombarded her with doggy kisses. Emma's family didn't own any official pets, just their horses and some chickens, but she immediately warmed up to him.

"Charlie likes you! I knew he would," cooed Auntie Willa.

"I like him, too! We've never had a dog," Emma replied, scratching Charlie behind the ears.

"Well you do now. Mi perro es tu perro!"

"What?"

"Oh that's just a little Spanish for you. It means 'my dog is your dog.' I can teach you a little while you're here if you'd like."

Emma didn't know that Auntie Willa could speak another language. She was impressed by how worldly her aunt was, but then remembered that focusing her attention on things like that is what drew Auntie Willa away from the church in the first place.

"Maybe, but I don't know what good Spanish would do me back home."

It was clear Auntie Willa didn't agree, but she refrained from pushing the matter.

"Why don't you get settled in your room? Maybe hang up some of the clothes you brought, take a shower, and I'll order up some Chinese food. You ever have Chinese food? Probably not, but you'll love it. I swear!"

"Okay," was all Emma could muster. She had only ever eaten what Mama or their neighbors had cooked for her. The idea of "ordering" food was as unfamiliar as "Chinese," but she was uncomfortable denying Auntie Willa's hospitality. She took her bag into the spare room and began to unpack before cautiously figuring out how to work the shower.

When she got out of the bathroom she found a warm looking pair of sweatpants and a baggy t-shirt waiting for her on her bed.

"I know you probably brought a nightgown with you," Auntie Willa yelled from the living room, "but trust me, there's nothing cozier than a hand-me-down pair of sweatpants that are too big for you."

Not one to protest, she pulled on the black pair of pants and the shirt that said "Chicago Marathon 2013" on the front and met Auntie Willa in the living room where a feast of little white boxes, black plastic containers, and a mountain of fortune cookies was waiting for her.

"I didn't know what you liked so I got a little bit of everything. Plus, I told them we were having a party so they'd give me extra fortune cookies. Dig in!" She handed Emma a plate, a pair of chopsticks, and a fork just in case.

Between surprisingly delicious bites of fried rice and sesame chicken, Emma asked her aunt about the t-shirt.

"Did you run a marathon, Auntie Willa?"

"Ha! I just bought ten pounds of Chinese food. What do you think? No, my ex-boyfriend gave me that shirt while we were dating."

Emma was suddenly uncomfortable about the idea of wearing a man's shirt, and Auntie Willa could see that.

"Don't worry, girly, he hasn't warn that shirt in years so it practically never belonged to him in the first place."

This reassured Emma enough that she continued to wear the shirt but now she had more questions.

"Auntie Willa, how many boyfriends have you had?"

"Well that depends. I've officially had three serious boyfriends, but I've casually dated quite a few more."

This took Emma aback. Mama met Papa at a Sunday evening sing and that was that. The girls at home almost always end up marrying the first boy who takes them home in his buggy. The idea that Auntie Willa had dated more than one man, had even worn their clothes, shocked her. She wondered how many other men's t-shirts she had in her closet, but she didn't dare ask.

"Wow," she replied, "I've never even held hands with a boy."

Auntie Willa chuckled kindly, "Well let's see what we can do about that, huh?"

This made Emma blush wildly and spoon too much rice into her mouth to keep from having to respond.

***

Auntie Willa wasted no time fulfilling her promise to take Emma to the planetarium. The very next day, after gently insisting that Emma borrow some more of her clothes and that she "leave the bonnet at home, girly!" they hopped in a cab and made their way to the museum.

The Adler Planetarium sat out on its own at the tip of a peninsula that jutted way out into Lake Michigan. Driving towards the impressive domed building gave Emma the same sensation as when she first saw the Chicago skyline. She couldn't wait to get inside to see where they kept all the stars, but after the cab dropped them off at the entrance Auntie Willa put her hand on Emma's shoulder to stop her from immediately sprinting up the stairs to the front doors.

"Hold up! Turn around first. Don't you want to see what I was talking about?"

Emma turned and saw the same skyline that awed her from a distance magnified and close enough to touch. That impressive massiveness that she felt fifty miles away was now right on top of her. The beautiful weight of the city was balanced on her small shoulders and she loved it. This feeling was enough to cause a small chip in Emma's resolve to return home, and this frightened her. She spun around on her heal, as if not being able to see the skyline made it not exist. She wasted no time climbing the stairs to the planetarium now. She relied on the familiarity of the stars to remind her of why she wanted to go home, but she didn't count on what else she would find inside.

***

After wandering around the exhibits for a while, taking in every fact about space, the stars, and especially the Sun that she could find, Auntie Willa suggested that they sit for a while and see a show. They decided on one called *Skywatch Live!* which showed how the night sky above Chicago would look if the city turned off all of its lights. This one interested Emma the most. She wanted to see how different the sky is here as opposed to at home.

Soon after they took their seats in the huge, domed theater the lights dimmed and the starry Chicago sky was projected above them. Emma had to stifle a gasp as every star she'd ever seen and more swirled above them. She was loath to admit it to herself, but it was almost more magical than the real night sky at home. Wrapped up in the tableau unfurling in front of her, she was caught off guard when a voice projected across the audience.

"Welcome, everybody! Thanks for coming out to see *Skywatch Live!* with me. My name's Nathan, and I'll be your night sky tour guide today."

Nathan had a pleasant voice, confident but not too rough. Emma thought he sounded like he had a sense of humor that he wasn't quite ready to share with the audience yet. Then she thought she shouldn't be thinking about this strange man's voice at all and tried her best to focus on the stars.

"Later on tonight, you'll probably be able to see Saturn even with all of the city lights. Do you want to hear a bad joke about Saturn?" A smattering of people in the audience cheered him on. "Okay, don't hate me for this. Why does Saturn have rings?"

"Why?" the audience, including Auntie Willa, happily asked.

"Because God liked it so he put a ring on it! Saturn is not a single lady."

He was met with a mixture of laughter and groans from the audience. Emma didn't really understand the joke but she found herself laughing anyways. There was something about the way Nathan said his joke was bad that made her feel like he actually thought the opposite. She could tell by his voice that he amused himself and she couldn't help but feel endeared by that.

"I told you it was terrible! Let's move on. I'm embarrassed," Nathan continued, but Emma knew he wasn't.

Emma tried as she might to focus on the show but Nathan's voice kept drawing her in. She wanted to know more things about him; what he looked like, if he liked Chinese food, did he want to hold her hand. Her cheeks flushed at that thought. He didn't even know she was in the same room as him, let alone if he'd be interested in *that*. More than that, she didn't even know who he was really, just the sound of his voice. Just as she began to talk herself out of these feelings for Nathan, he concluded the show and told everyone to come see him if they had any questions about the show. This chance to talk to him face-to-face squashed all of the doubts in her mind as she scrambled to think of a question.

"Auntie Willa, I've got a question for Nathan. Do you mind if we stop and ask?"

Auntie Willa had a hunch about Emma's true intentions.

"Sure thing. I actually have to use the ladies' so how about we meet by the sun when you're through?"

"Great, thanks!" Emma replied before speeding away full of nervous energy.

Emma tried to slow down to give herself time to think of the perfect question but before she knew it she was standing in front of a tall brunette man with a kind face and a nametag that said "Nathan."

"Hey!" he greeted her, "Did you enjoy the show? Gotta question for me?"

Emma nodded and asked the first thing that came into her mind, "Why was your joke funny?"

Nathan was not expecting this question, but he hid his surprise behind an understanding smile.

"The joke about Saturn? It was a reference to a Beyonce song where she talks about some guy who wouldn't marry her. So, I guess the joke's funny for that reason, but also can you imagine God marrying a planet?" This made him laugh, but only confused Emma.

"Who's Beyonce?"

"Who's Beyonce? What are you, an alien?" he replied incredulously, but not unkindly.

Emma picked up on his playfulness and said, "No, at least I don't think so. I grew up out in the country where there isn't much music except for in church. I guess that might as well be another planet compared to here."

It turned out more than just his own jokes could make Nathan laugh. He let out a whoop and wasn't shy about it or his feelings.

'I like you!" he said, "What's your name?"

"Emma," she replied, her signature blush swept across he face, but the traditional shyness that usually came along with it wasn't there. In fact, she had never felt more confident. Against all odds, and especially against her own rules for herself, she liked him too. She felt a small pang of worry about what consequences she might face for these feelings, but she pushed them away at least for this moment.

Nathan stuck his hand out in front of him and said, "Nice to meet you, Emma. You already know my name, but would you like to know more about me?"

"Absolutely," she said as she excitedly shook his hand. This was the first thing she felt confident of since she got here. It was only after giving Nathan Auntie Willa's phone number that she realized they had held hands, and in that moment she felt more alive than any day she had back home. Emma was in love and terrified.

***

Emma didn't have to wait long by the phone before Nathan called. She and Auntie Willa talked about him that night after they got home from the planetarium. She was excited for Emma, but warned her not to get her hopes to high about some guy she just met. Emma wanted to explain that he was more than that, but didn't know how to put it into words. She was having a hard time understanding these feelings herself. Luckily, Auntie Willa was a young girl in love once, too, and understood that sometimes these things need to run their course.

"Hey! Is this Emma from the planetarium?"

Emma had made sure that Auntie Willa gave her a complete lesson on how to use the phone well before she actually had to answer it.

"It is! Is this Nathan, also from the planetarium?"

"Sure is. Now let me get straight to the point, because I'm sure you've heard enough of my disembodied voice. I want to take you to dinner. Do you eat on your planet?"

Emma couldn't help but giggle girlishly.

"Yes, of course we eat!"

"Perfect. I'll come by your place around six. I'm thinking it's about time you tried classic Chicago deep dish pizza."

"We definitely don't have that where I'm from, but it sounds great!"

"See you then, then. Buh-bye Emma."

"Goodbye!"

Emma couldn't believe what she was about to do. In her wildest dreams back home she never thought she would be going on a date with a man in the city, let alone enjoy it. Auntie Willa was right. Chicago was changing her and it was starting to become difficult not to think it's for the better.

***

Nathan took Emma on a handful more dates over the next few weeks before they finally came back to the planetarium. In that time she had learned his favorite color (red), how many siblings he had (two), his favorite book (*A Brief History of Time*), and he learned all that and more about her (sky blue, one, The Bible). But she couldn't help but feel that he was keeping something from her. He was almost unnervingly forthright with her, to the point where she felt like she could ask him anything, but when she asked why he worked at the planetarium he grew solemn. This only lasted a moment before he coolly replied, "because I love teaching people about space!" but she could tell that wasn't the real answer. It made her uncomfortable that she knew there was something Nathan was actively keeping from her, but she was so happily in love that she didn't want to push him away by prying.

At the planetarium, Nathan had arranged a private, after hours tour for the two of them. This was the first time she had been alone with him and that made her nervous, but excited. Nathan had been nothing but a gentleman to her the entire time they were dating. He could tell she had some reservations about becoming physical with him, and he respected that. They often held hands in the park and always hugged goodbye when he dropped her off at home, but had yet to kiss. He knew about her religion and the fact that she was only here for a couple more weeks, but every time she anxiously brought up the fact that their relationship had an expiration date he just held her close and told her not to worry about anything but that exact moment. Each time he held her, Emma could never see the sad smile Nathan had on his face.

They made the same rounds through the exhibits as Emma and Auntie Willa did the first time she came here, but this time there was no one else around and Nathan told her secrets about different artifacts on display. She loved every second of it, but couldn't help wondering about the one secret that he wouldn't share with her.

Eventually they made their way to the same theater where they first met. A starry sky was projected above them and on the floor at the front of the theater Nathan had arranged a romantic picnic, complete with different cheese, candles, and a bottle of champagne. Emma was so overwhelmed at the sight of this gesture that she kissed him right there in the doorway. She hadn't planned to, but her nervousness slipped out of her body the moment Nathan's lips touched hers. They were as soft as down, but the pressure he put behind them made it seem like they might never part. Nathan softly grabbed the back of Emma's neck with one hand and held her waist with the other. She instinctively wrapped her arms around his neck and pulled his body as close to hers as she could without fusing them together.

This kiss was like seeing the city for the first time. It was like the first bite of Chinese food. It was lying on the grass looking at the stars. It was sunrise.

When they finally parted she could see that Nathan was silently crying.

"Nathan! What's wrong? Should I not have done that?"

"No!" he said chuckling through the tears, "You definitely should have done that." He sighed and touched her cheek. "I've got to tell you something. Will you sit down with me?"

Emma felt a knot in her stomach as Nathan lead her to the blanket surrounded by candles. He popped open the champagne, poured them both a glass, and said, "You're beautiful."

"Is that what you had to tell me?"

"It's one thing, but it's not *the* thing."

The way he said *"the* thing" made it sound like some sort of storybook monster.

"Just tell me. You're making me nervous."

"Emma... I'm dying. Like, really, incurably, probably quickly dying."

Emma couldn't say anything. At first, she thought this was just another of his bad jokes but it became clear by the tears welling in his eyes that he was serious. She threw herself into his lap and cried with him, spilling the champagne onto the blanket. They held each other quietly for a while before Emma finally spoke.

"I love you."

"I love you, too"

In that moment nothing else mattered to Emma. Her home, her family, God were all forgotten as she lay there on the floor with this surprising man that wasn't even supposed to be a part of her life. Now he felt like a permanent fixture. That night she decided she could ask for forgiveness later. They had found somehow each other in an infinite universe and that was a gift more precious and unique than any other. They made love in the theater that night under the stars.

***

Emma stayed in the city just long enough to go to Nathan's funeral. She wore a simple black dress that Auntie Willa lent her. The funeral was held in a Catholic church filled with ornamentation, extravagant robes, and subdued singing. She couldn't help but feel that Nathan would have wanted something simpler, more light hearted, but who was she to say? Her first love had come and gone like a comet. She broke her own rules, as well as God's and had nothing left to show for it. When the priest called everyone up to take communion, Emma just shook her head and cried. He understood, said a blessing over her, and sent her back to her seat. She didn't understand the tradition, but felt oddly comforted by it.

When she got back to Auntie Willa's she couldn't talk at all. Emma went straight to bed and shut the door. Tomorrow she was supposed to return home. She lay awake in bed for hours thinking about if that's what she really wanted after all. Around five in the morning she gave up trying to sleep and started to pack. She left the blinds open that night and soon her room was filled with pink and orange light. The sun rising over Lake Michigan painted the sky and made the water look like light. She watched the top of the sun peek over the horizon and slowly fill the sky. "This is a new beginning," she reminded herself, "Not just for me, but for Nathan, too."

The sight of something so familiar, but all together new gave Emma the answers she needed. Looking out over the painted lake, she knew she would be okay.

END

BE GOOD, MY STARLIGHT : AN AMISH ROMANCE

NATALIE SALEM

Chapter One

"Be good, my starlight, I love you," Naomi said gently. She leaned down and hugged her son tight. He was just barely five, but was now old enough to start classes.

His golden hair looked nothing like her brown locks, his brown eyes were so dark compared to her green ones. He was hers, though, despite appearances. He was her entire world, and she knew that she'd do anything to make sure he was happy and unaware of the hardships she faced. He kissed her cheek, and then immediately ran off with a couple other boys to start their lessons.

Her family was setting her up with a stranger.

He was supposedly a good man.

Naomi was yet to see that, she knew that he'd be at her home with her family by the time she returned from her son's school. She knew he was a hard worker, that he had a daughter, and that he was ten years older than her.

She wasn't keen on him being thirty, but she knew that, given her circumstances, he was starting to look like the only option.

Naomi looked back at the school house as she started back home. The elderly teacher, Mister Lapp, was ushering in the last of the children, and she watched him with interest.

He had a job in this community.

A place.

Nobody would look at him and wonder why he was alone, or who he was.

She wished for a life so easy.

The soft summer grass gave way under her shoes as she headed back to the main street. Golden light, radiating off a bright morning sun, brought her entire village to life and motion around her.

Everyone was pleased to greet one another, everyone was starting their day and jobs.

Except her.

Nobody greeted her as she walked through the village, she kept her eyes averted in fear of any stray staring. She felt like how she imagined English must feel when they come into town with their shiny cars.

Different.

Unwanted.

She tried to distract herself, and remind herself of things she knew of Vernon.

He was 30, owned land as a farmer, was a widower. He had a daughter who was nearing seven and was in desperate need of a mother since she'd be out of school within the next handful of years.

Vernon sounded respectable.

Sounded like her only chance.

Still, as Naomi reached her family's home, she couldn't help but feel a pang of regret. A marriage without love wasn't much of a marriage. A marriage of convenience would help her family, help her reputation, help her life, but she'd still hurt. She'd still feel out of place and unhappy. She was sure of it. Naomi let herself in, pulled off her black bonnet, and reassured herself that this would be fine: she needed to think of her family and son first.

"Naomi, are you home?" her father called from the kitchen. She could smell that her mother was cooking something, despite the fact that they all just had breakfast.

"I am, father," she replied, following his voice. The kitchen was large, but as she walked in, and felt all eyes upon her, it felt very tight and small.

A man she'd never seen before was standing in the corner sipping what smelled like very dark coffee. He was taller than her, his face shaven to show he was unmarried. She noted that he was handsome, that he looked sturdy and strong, but she felt no strong pull to him.

"This is Vernon Miller," her father introduced, motioning to the man. "We were talking about the idea of marriage between you two," he said flatly.

Naomi felt her heart drop.

She knew that this was her family's goal, but she'd thought she'd been given the chance to court first. She looked to her mother for help, but her mother just cast her eyes aside and turned back to cooking.

"It's good to meet you," Vernon said, standing and offering his hand to her. The action felt incredibly intimate, given what was just said, but she took his hand and shook it softly anyways. His grip was firm, his hand was warm.

She didn't want this.

Still, she knew better than to be rude.

"Nice to meet you as well," she replied.

"Can I drive you home from church on Sunday?" he offered. Naomi almost laughed, that was the kind of courting only teenagers did, and he was almost twice the age he should be to ask.

Her father gave her a stern look, though.

"I would like that," she replied. "Would you like more coffee?"

"I would be very thankful for more," he answered, not taking his eyes off of hers. A blush flooded her cheeks from the attention, and Naomi quickly took his mug to get out of his sight.

He talked with her father comfortably about the farm work, about how much land he owned. It discomforted her to realize he was the same space in age from her parents as he was to her. She couldn't imagine her mother or father marrying someone so much younger than they were.

Naomi gave him his coffee, and he stopped to spare her a smile before he continued talking. He was trying harder to impress her parents than he was to impress her, she didn't mind. She was almost complemented to think that he actually wanted her.

Soon he was leaving, and she was set to work in the garden to keep it weeded and watered.

She was sure if she set her mind to it she could love him.

She was 20, the age most girls would be able to choose if they wanted to leave the church or not. The age most women would have dozens of offers and freedom to choose as they wished.

Yet she had to scramble and grab to get the one offer she did.

Her family loved her, cared about her, and they were trying to make sure that she lived happily. They didn't want to see her grow old and alone, with just her son in her life.

They didn't want her to have to spend her entire life in their home.

A plane passed overhead, and Naomi craned her neck and let herself watch it. She couldn't help but wonder, if her situation had been different and she were English instead, would she have been happier with that life?

She'd had the choice taken from her, though.

Naomi had sworn to the church and was going to live her whole life happily being a part of it.

She loved her son, John, would do anything to protect him and raise him well. She'd fallen pregnant with him at just fifteen.

Fallen from grace in the community when she gave birth to him at age fifteen.

She'd had many friends, had a fun life, before her pregnancy.

She'd gone to sings to meet boys, had been courted by two, and yet one poor decision had left her ostracized from everyone but family.

Sighing as the plane went out of sight, Naomi felt resigned.

She'd make herself fall in love with him.

Almost six years since she was found to be pregnant had passed, almost six years she had spent unwanted.

He wanted her.

He was interested in her.

She couldn't see herself getting another chance like this, and she didn't want to let down her family.

She'd love him eventually, she was sure of it.

Chapter Two

The next day, a bright and sunny Tuesday, Naomi and her son arrived to the school to find it closed. A sign hung on the door, white crisp paper with clear handwriting. When she could finally get close enough, through the gaggle of mothers and children reading it, she was shocked.

Mister Lapp, the elderly school teacher, had passed in the night from a heart attack.

Naomi walked John home, disturbed and unsure of how to explain it to him. He didn't have to deal with death yet, her parents, and her parent's parents, were all alive still.

She hadn't expected him to pass, then again she never really saw death coming for anyone. Once someone got to a certain age they moved back in with one of their children to live out their retirement in comfort. Most people didn't work until they died.

The rest of her day was spent more heavily considering marrying Vernon. If she passed he would be much more able to take care of her son than her aging parents or her two older siblings who had left the church.

The next day, despite her heart telling her the school would still be closed, she walked her son the same path she did most days.

Nobody else with children were about, nobody seemed to be heading to the school. She felt foolish at first, before realizing someone was in the school house.

The sign was gone from the door.

"Hello?" she asked, holding her son's hand as she peeked inside the schoolhouse doors. There was a young man at the front of the classroom, flipping through a book. He looked up at the sound of her voice and smiled.

"Hello! Please, come in," he said, motioning to her and John. She couldn't help but notice the rest of the room was empty besides them, usually there were at least twenty children in class every day.

"Where is everyone?" she asked, surprised.

"I was just asking myself the same question," he smiled sadly, looking pointedly around. "They may be taking a day to grieve," he offered as an explanation.

"Must be," she murmured, trying not to notice how handsome the man was. He had a strong jawline, but sweet blue eyes. His cheekbones were sharp, and they led her attention to his soft looking lips. His face was clean shaven. Unmarried.

His looks were hard to ignore.

"I'll call it an off day, then," he sighed, leaning back against his desk.

"Are you from the area?" she found herself asking. She was sure she'd know if she'd seen him before. He was too attractive to be forgettable, and too close-looking to her age for him to have not been to the same sings and gatherings as her.

"I've been caught," he joked. He was lighthearted, warm. She was caught off guard and found herself savoring it. Not many people in her village even acted like she existed anymore. Years of shame had left her starving for any kind of positive attention. "I'm from a town in Idaho, I wanted a move to see what the rest of our churches had to offer," he explained.

"Have you taught before?"

"Mommy can we go?" her son interrupted before the new man could answer.

"John, I need you to have patience," she said softly, leaning down to his height. He looked slightly scolded, but sat down in one of the chairs and waited.

"He's so well behaved," the new teacher said, watching him.

"Thank you," she said gently. A child who misbehaved was a bad mark on the parent and she knew it. A compliment on her son was a compliment to her.

"Of course," he replied. "I'm Eli," he walked towards her, offering his hand.

"Naomi," she said softly, accepting his hand and shaking it. She felt shocks go through her body at the contact. What was this feeling?

He let go of her hand slowly, and she immediately missed the contact.

"I taught grades kindergarten through third for a year in Idaho," he said, answering the question she'd asked earlier.

"I see," Naomi made herself answer.

She wanted to say more, to ask more, but she forced herself to have some control.

"We should go," she said after a moment, looking down at her son who was starting to drift off to sleep. "Thank you, I'll make sure word gets out that there will be class tomorrow," she said gently, smiling.

"That would be very kind," he smiled. "Have a good day," he offered.

"You also," she nodded, leading her son out.

She'd found him attractive.

More than that, she corrected herself, she was attracted to him.

Quietly she admonished herself as they headed back to her parent's home. She knew better than to seek the attention of men. She knew that it never worked out well for her.

Yet she found herself glancing back at the schoolhouse to see if she could catch a glimpse of the new teacher.

He was looking out the window back at them.

Color fled onto her cheeks and she looked back towards their path. He was handsome, educated. He had a job that would leave him being an important part of the community.

Eli.

She repeated his name in her mind.

It was a common name, but it felt special attached to him. She regretted not learning his last name, and as she had this thought more guilt fled her heart.

If he knew anything about her.

About her situation.

He wouldn't have been so sweet to her, she was sure of it.

Eli was kind because he was a teacher, because it was his job to be, not because he was interested in her. She took a deep breath and reminded herself that her family had picked a very suitable man for her anyways.

This was just cold feet.

Her family had laid a very straight line for her, and if she followed it she could be very happy.

Vernon was an older man, but he had lived there his whole life, had roots in the community. Eli was attractive and closer to her age, but he would want to start from scratch with a respectable wife.

Not with her.

Naomi scooped up her son and carried him the rest of the way home in her arms, trying not to admit to herself how excited she was to see Eli the next day.

Chapter Three

The next morning there were many people at the school.

Eli was talking, and smiling, and being more than friendly with the other mothers who had come. Naomi took it as confirmation that he really was just being nice to her.

She didn't need to read into him too much.

Tightening her bonnet a little she walked John the rest of the way to the school.

"Miss Naomi," he greeted her, his smile warm and welcoming.

"I don't think I caught your last name," she replied, also smiling.

"Troyer," he answered, a friendly sound in his voice.

"Do take care of my boy, Mister Troyer," she said softly.

"He won't be too much trouble," Eli replied, shaking his head and smiling.

Naomi spent the rest of the walk home memorizing his smile.

That evening she got to thank him for his care, again.

His face stayed in her mind.

"You're smiling a lot today," he mother commented, the water on the stove started to boil. "Is it that you're keen to the idea of Mister Miller now?" she asked. There were no notes of teasing in her voice, it was an honest question.

"I'm keen to the idea of marriage," Naomi replied, keeping her answer vague.

She didn't want her mother to know.

The next day was Friday.

She tried to make excuses for herself as to why they were arriving at the school house a full twenty minutes later. The warm muffins in her basket were enough evidence to prove them all wrong.

"Mister Troyer?" she knocked on the schoolhouse door and peeked in. He was looking through papers at his desk. At their intrusion he glanced at the wind-up clock on his desk.

"You're early," he said, it wasn't accusing or confused, he was almost pleased sounding.

"I thought I'd welcome you properly to the community," she offered, bringing forward the muffins.

"They smell very good, thank you," he said, standing to meet them halfway to the door.

"Sorry about being so early, I was up early this morning and lost track of my time," she apologized as he accepted the basket.

"No, please, you're fine," he replied, shaking his head. "I haven't eaten today and these are a welcome sight," he added.

She went home that day feeling like she was floating.

Friday turned into Saturday, and then soon it was Sunday and Vernon was greeting her at church.

She'd almost forgotten about him.

Now, after she'd spent so many days getting glimpses and small moments with Eli at the schoolhouse, Vernon seemed very different to her.

He was older, more of a man. She knew thirty wasn't old by any standards, but Eli was her age. Vernon seemed more stern suddenly, and less interesting. He nodded to her, cordially, properly, and then she sat with her family.

The service was a memorial to Mister Lappe, the school teacher.

Guilt flooded Naomi again, it was her norm. She'd not mourned the teacher, she was too busy being interested in the new one.

In Eli.

In her interest and attraction, she'd lost her morals.

Naomi bowed her head, listening to the sermon, and started to pray for forgiveness. Regardless of how lonely she'd been, she didn't need to become selfish and thoughtless.

Vernon was an actual choice.

Her only choice.

Whatever she was thinking was interest from Eli was nothing more than courtesy from a teacher to his student's parent. She knew this, she needed to keep it in mind. If he knew anything about her, if he had the slightest inkling about how the town viewed her, he wouldn't be so friendly.

Flirting towards him, paying him any attention, was empty and useless.

She needed to get that through her head.

Newly resigned, she sat through the rest of the service and listened carefully. When church finally wound down to an end her family left her behind without mention, leading a sleepy John away for a nap. Naomi wished she could go with them and not have to talk to Vernon.

He appeared to her through the crowd, a small smile on his mouth, and she followed him to his buggy. Vernon was thoughtful, helping her up into the buggy, carrying on comfortable conversation about her family and his work.

He was sweet.

It made it worse.

She couldn't help but feel like if he were rude, if there was anything about him that she didn't like, she'd have an out.

He gave her no excuses.

He was kind, gentle, understanding. He was everything that, before knowing Eli, she would have wanted in a man. Her family had a keen eye in choosing him to be introduced to her, and she appreciated that. She wished he held her interest as well as Eli had.

"Your mother invited me for dinner Tuesday night," he said idly as they neared her home. "I wanted to check that you also want me there," he added, turning to her.

"We would all love to have you there," she said, not meaning it.

Her parents would love to have him there, and she would love to make her parents happy, regardless of what that meant for her.

Chapter Four

Monday came and Naomi didn't pause to greet Eli. She didn't make eye contact with him or smile to him as she dropped off her son.

She'd convinced herself that if she was going to rid herself of affection for him, the best way to do it was to stop letting herself talk warmly to him. Any interaction would be too much, and she wouldn't let it happen.

At least, she thought she wouldn't.

Six hours later, when she returned to pick up John, Eli asked her to stay after the class cleared out. She agreed to, feeling her heart race as he said her name. She beat down the feelings, but they just simmered under the surface instead. Her traitorous heart didn't care about what was right or pure, it just wanted his attention.

"Has John done something wrong?" she asked as the last of the children left with their mothers.

"No, never, he's a model student," Eli replied, shaking his head. He gathered the papers his students had left behind from their desks. "May I step outside with you while he stays in here?" Eli asked, making eye contact with her. His expression was apologetic, and her heart warmed over it.

She adored him.

"Did I anger you?" he asked as they stepped out. The day was overcast, the strong winds above pushed the clouds at an alarmingly high speed. There would be a storm by morning.

"No," she was honest.

"Are you well?" he asked, he was obviously concerned. She needed to clear the air or it would torture her forever. If she just leapt to Vernon's side as his wife without ever knowing if there was a chance with Eli, she'd never forgive herself.

"Why do you pay me attention?" she asked, the words tumbled out of her mouth like heavy stones.

He looked taken aback for just a moment. "I find you interesting, you're very kind and I want to return the favor," he answered.

"Nothing more?" she asked, unsure. His expression faltered for a moment.

"That's not entirely true," he sighed, leaning against the schoolhouse. He glanced in to look at John for a moment. "I find my thoughts stay with you even when you're not here," he admitted. "At first, I pushed it aside because I assumed you were married because of John," he said. "One of the other mothers mentioned you were single and lived with your parents, so I felt no guilt in talking to you."

"Even with a child out of wedlock?" she asked.

He looked uneasy for a moment. "It's something I would have to heavily consider before courting you."

"You'd consider courting me?" Naomi was even more surprised by this bit of information.

"I would at some point," he said, honestly. She read it as a 'no' since it wasn't a 'yes.'

"I don't mean to make you uncomfortable," she replied, her heart dropping into her stomach. "I just," she sighed. "I misunderstood your intentions and I'm terribly sorry."

"Don't be," Eli said, shaking his head. "I'm not sure what I feel for you, I need to reflect and pray on it, can you give me a week?" he asked, his eyes were warm and sweet.

"Of course, take your time," Naomi answered, as if she weren't being rushed to marry Vernon.

She gathered John and they left.

John was happy to talk about how much he enjoyed Eli's lessons better, that they were more interesting than how Mister Lapp had taught them. Naomi scolded him for speaking ill of someone, if if they're dead, but was pleased to know her son took a shining to Eli. He hadn't even shown a little bit of interest in Vernon.

Tuesday morning when she took her son to school, she didn't talk to Eli or make eye contact with him. It was the same when she picked her son up after.

She didn't want to seem like she was trying to seduce him, didn't want to sway Eli into something he didn't want.

That night, Vernon was at their home for dinner. He and her father spoke about the weather, and of crops for the year. Naomi tried to pay attention and be as sweet and appealing as possible.

He could never know that she was on the verge of crying because of another man. It would just add more shame to who she was. Her mother stopped before cleaning dishes to invite him for dinner on Friday as well, and he accepted.

Her parents were getting her further and further into this man's life.

What would happen if by some miracle Eli accepted her and they started courting? Would her parents hate her for yanking them around?

Would they ever forgive her?

Nightfall found her sobbing in the garden after she set John to bed. Crickets filled the air with their noise, and she tried to distract herself with them.

She's only fallen pregnant with John because she'd kept secrets from her parents. She fell in love with a boy, and he tried to introduce her to all that he knew of the English. How wild and adventurous their lives could be, how different it was from their own world.

Naomi became swept up in those ideas.

She went further with him, becoming intimate, not entirely knowing what she was doing. Her mother had only ever said, "never take your dress off around anyone else,".

She fell pregnant.

Then, during the boy's Rumspringa, he'd left.

Left the church, left his family, left her.

Her parents were furious, they had expected him to marry her and be forced into staying with the church- but they couldn't take that choice away from him.

He left.

She never got to fully enjoy her Rumspringa because of him.

Never got to finish being young.

She was forced immediately into motherhood, into following that path, before she even got to see the world outside of her community. The people around her looked down on her for being a single mother so young, she felt every glare and sneer that had struck her over the last five years. Her shame was too painful.

All of this because she kept a secret from her parents.

Naomi wiped her face, but the tears kept falling.

"Naomi, what is it?" her mother's soft voice said from behind. Naomi jumped a little, startled, but then began to cry more at the sight of her.

"I think I love another man, mother," she explained. "He's considering courting me, and asked a week to think it over," she confessed it quickly, the words poured out of her like water.

"Why didn't you tell me?" her mother asked, sitting beside her she wrapped her arm around Naomi.

"I'm worried I'm being selfish again," she answered. Her mother didn't respond immediately, just sat their and held her softly.

"He sounds like a thoughtful man for waiting to think about it, and you sound like you've been thinking it over too," her mother answered. "I'll ask your father to tell Mister Miller to come next week instead of Friday, and if this other man asks to court you, we'll consider him instead," she explained.

"Are you sure?" Naomi asked, wiping her face.

"We just want you to be married and happy like we are, that's all," her mother explained.

"Thank you," Naomi sighed, ready and hopeful for Eli to give her an answer.

The rest of the week slid by like thick tar.

She tried to avoid looking at him at all, but kept catching her eyes flicking over to him and watching him. She wasn't happy that she had to see him twice a day, and started dreading taking John to and from school. Every time she saw Eli and he didn't approach her with an answer it felt like a more definite 'no'.

Sunday came, and he'd still not said anything.

Vernon offered to drive her home, and she let him, but she didn't say a word the whole way home. He didn't seem to notice. Unlike Eli, who immediately pointed out that she was acting odd, Vernon just kept talking about how he wanted to raise a new barn.

She was exhausted of him, and was starting to loathe how secure he seemed in marrying her.

***

Finally, it was Monday morning.

She wore her black bonnet, and her favorite dress and cape.

It wasn't flashy. Nothing she, or anyone around her, wore was, but it was her favorite shade of blue, and she felt lovely in it. She left early with John, so that Eli wouldn't have to say anything in front of anyone, and tried to keep a lid on her energy.

When she arrived he was behind his desk, writing.

"Sorry we're early, is it alright if I leave him here?" she asked. These were the first words she'd said to him in a week.

"That's fine," he answered, barely looking up from his papers.

It was a no, then.

Naomi nodded, then turned and bit her lip as she started to walk home. He didn't want to court her. Eli had no interest in her. Her heart ached, and she tried to remind herself that she still had Vernon as a possibility, she wouldn't be alone.

Somehow, that made it worse.

Chapter Five

She didn't tell her mother his answer when she got home.

She didn't start the laundry, like she did every Monday. She didn't do anything but go to her room and kneel to pray.

Naomi wanted answers.

She needed to know what to do next, where to take her path. Should she just give up on any other men and marry Vernon now that he was the only choice? Should she stay single and hope another eventually notices her?

Both options sounded terrible, but they were her only two.

The way he didn't even look her in the face burned at her heart again, and she started praying harder, looking for guidance between her tears. She didn't want to be alone for the rest of her life, but she also didn't want to end up in a loveless marriage. Her week of talking to and falling for Eli had been so warm and good, and although it was short lived she wanted to feel that way more. She wanted to feel loved.

Her mother came in to gather the sheets, starting the laundry since Naomi hadn't yet, and paused for a moment.

"It's been a week, today, and I think his answer is 'no,'" Naomi explained, standing up from kneeling.

"Then it's a blessing you also have Vernon in your life," her mother said, patting Naomi's hair softly for a moment, like she did when her daughter was younger. "We love you and will be here for you for as long as you want us," her mother explained.

Naomi knew that wouldn't last forever.

Her mother would need to retire eventually, would need someone to take care of her and offer her a home. Both of Naomi's older siblings left the church and wouldn't be able to offer that. If Naomi stayed single there was no way she could support them.

She'd have to marry Vernon. Marrying him was the only way to be sure that she could properly thank them for all they'd done for her. The only way to show God, and the church, that she truly was thankful for all she had.

"Tomorrow I'll tell father I'll marry Vernon if he'll have me. Today my heart needs to mourn," Naomi said, hugging her mother close.

"We're proud of you Naomi," her mother said. "We love you and John, we're glad to have you in our home," she explained.

Naomi cleaned her face and then set to helping with the laundry, letting it distract her.

The day passed more quickly now, and she almost lost track of the time. An hour before she was supposed to leave to pick John up from school, her son came running out to the garden to her.

"John! What are you doing here?" she asked, alarmed.

"Mister Troyer let us out early," he answered, hugging against her leg.

"Who walked you home?" she leaned down and looked him over, ensuring he was fine. His golden hair was so much like Eli's that she could almost see him as his son.

"Mister Troyer," he answered. "He told all the others that it was a short day," he went on. Then John began to babble about a math problem he was able to solve, but Naomi was completely distracted.

Why hadn't he told her it was a short day?

Why did he walk her son home?

Naomi stood quickly, looking over her dress and making sure that the soap hadn't soaked it. Taking John's hand in hers, she headed back into her parent's home.

There were voices in the main room of the house, and she followed through the kitchen to them.

Eli was sitting on a couch opposite her parents, and was talking to them comfortably. Naomi's heart was beating out of her chest, suddenly and strong.

He was here.

He was here and smiling at her.

She smiled back chastely, remembering herself, and sat down beside her mother. John kissed her goodbye and ran off to his room to do his homework.

"I want to court your daughter," Eli said flatly. "I know that usually this is done in other ways, that it would be kept quietly, but I learned this last week that Vernon was wanting her hand, and so I don't have the option to stay quiet." He watched over her parents carefully. The words caught Naomi by surprise and her whole body felt like it was buzzing.

He wanted to court her! She'd been resigned to being stuck marrying Vernon for her parent's future security, and now here was Eli. She knew she could so easily love him, she was already most of the way there, and they'd be happy together.

Naomi's mother exchanged a look with her, as if confirming this was the man she had cried over. When Naomi nodded, her mother turned to Naomi's father and murmured something softly to him.

His demeanor changed just slightly into a softer one.

"Do you own land?" her father asked, sitting back in his seat.

"I do, it has a home on it and room for a garden," Eli replied.

"Would your end intent be marriage?" her father asked. Naomi's heart pounded at the question.

"It would be," Eli didn't hesitate in saying his.

Naomi's heart was soaring. She tried to remember what prayers she had said before so that she could thank God for answering each of them. She wanted so much to just walk across the room and kiss Eli and say that she wanted the same.

The room was quiet, though.

She began to realize it had been a couple minutes since Eli answered, and her father still hadn't said anything. She turned to look at her father, gray seeping into his once-red beard, and watched his expression. He looked like he was seriously considering things.

"I see no problem in it," her father answered finally, breathing out slowly. "Just be true to her," he added.

"I will be," Eli replied.

He stayed a little longer and spoke casually with her father, looking over to Naomi every few moments like she was made of the stars themselves.

Nightfall began to near, and her mother offered for him to stay for dinner, but he declined and said he had to go over the tests.

"Naomi will walk you out then," her father said, heading to the kitchen with his wife.

Naomi's cheeks colored at the idea that her parents were leaving them alone. They stood together and headed to the front door slowly, their arms brushing.

"I'm sorry I didn't talk to you properly this morning," he said as they walked. "I was nervous to say it, to let it out, but I needed your family's permission first," he explained. "If I had spoken to you for more than a second I would have asked you to court me," he said, he was almost laughing.

"I'm so pleased you want to court me," it felt like an understatement, but she had to say something. "I like you very much," she admitted. They stood there, comfortable in each others silence, for a couple minutes as the evening's crickets began to pick up.

"I look forward to seeing you in the morning," he said gently, turning to her. "I always do," a smile was on his mouth.

"I do also," she replied.

He leaned towards her, and she met him halfway.

The kiss was gentle and sweet. His lips sent sparks through hers and in that moment she could see their future together.

A marriage with love.

Everything she'd ever wanted.

END

KAYLA

MONICA MARKS

It was Kayla's favorite time of year and when she woke that morning, she inhaled deeply, absorbing the nostalgic feeling which the onset of autumn brought along.

It is time for harvest and engagement announcements, she thought happily, swinging her long legs off the single mattress and scurrying to the window to stare into to endless farmland. The smallest frost had settled overnight but there was no cause for concern; the sunshine was fighting to warm the October day already and it was just past dawn. She tried to ignore the near exhaustion in her bones and stretched, willing herself to wake up.

I slept more than enough, she reasoned with her weary body. *There is no reason for me to be so tired.*

She told herself that the crisp fall air would invigorate her.

"Kayla!"

Her younger sister, Hannah threw open the door to her bedroom and folded her small arms across her chest.

"Haven't you dressed yet? It is almost seven o'clock!"

"Haven't you learned to knock yet? You are almost eight years old," Kayla replied haughtily. The sisters stared at each other before bursting into laughter.

"I am coming, Hannah," she assured the child. "There is time for breakfast and to walk to school."

Hannah smiled and Kayla clapped her hands.

"You lost another tooth!" she declared, rushing forward to examine her sister's mouth. "Let me see."

Hannah opened her mouth obligingly and the older sister patted her cheek.

"Go show *Daed* now," she instructed. "I will be along in a moment."

Hannah turned to leave Kayla, rushing down the steps toward the kitchen and Kayla hurried to change.

Hannah was not wrong; she had slept in again. It seemed to be happening with more frequency and Kayla had first believed the change of weather had been affecting her but suddenly she was not so certain.

I must eat better, she chided herself, slipping into a dark brown work dress and fastening an apron atop her skirt. *Autumn is not the time to waste time sleeping when Daed needs help with harvest and winter preparations. If you are so tired when the days are still long, what will you be like in two months?*

She padded across the threshold and into the corridor, trying to recall what needed to be done that morning. Canning needed to be started, the hay baled, pickling, jams...the list was endless as always and Kayla began to form a list in her mind in order of importance.

Slipping down the stairs, Kayla was suddenly overwhelmed by a wave of dizziness. She clutched the bannister, blood draining from her face as she tried to gather her bearings.

Oh Gotte, I do not have the luxury of being sick, she warned herself, willing a feeling of normalcy to come but in seconds, her legs had buckled and to her horror, Kayla tumbled down the remaining three steps onto the landing.

Not again! She thought, horrified, knowing that her family would witness her embarrassment this time. It was the third fainting spell she had experienced in two weeks but gratefully, her father and sister had not seen the others.

As spots of black and red danced before her eyes, she opened her mouth to moan but she began to lose consciousness as Hannah came running into the foyer, their father in tow.

The last thing she recalled before the world went dark was her small sister screaming.

When she woke, Jeremiah Roth stood praying over her, his eyes closed but even without reading the expression in his gentle blue irises, Kayla could see the concern in his face.

"*Daed*?" she called weakly, struggling to sit up against the bed. She realized she had been put back in her room, tucked in snugly among blankets.

"Oh, Kayla!" Jeremiah gasped, his lids flying open at the sound of her voice. "You must remain still. I have asked the Fishers to call for Dr. Imhoff."

"I am fine, *Daed*," Kayla protested. "It was nothing, I am sure. It happens sometimes."

"How many times?" Jeremiah demanded, his cornflower blue eyes wide with shock. "Why did you not tell me before?"

"It is no cause for alarm. Cancel the doctor!" Kayla groaned.

"Hush, *liebchen*," he insisted, pointing at the bed. "You will remain here until the doctor has seen you."

"We haven't time for this," Kayla insisted, attempting to rise again. "We have much to do."

"I am your father," Jeremiah growled with uncharacteristic sternness. "You will do as you are told. The harvest can wait."

Kayla settled back, blinking.

"All right, *Daed*," she relented. "I will wait but the Dr. Imhoff will tell you there is nothing wrong."

"I would rather hear it from him," Jeremiah replied. "He is the one with the medical degree after all."

He turned to the bedside and produced a glass of water.

"Drink this. I will wait downstairs Jonah."

"Where is Hannah?"

"Lydia Fisher has taken her to school. You mustn't worry, Kayla. All is tended to this morning. Your job is to rest."

He turned to leave the room before Kayla could form another argument, leaving her to stare at the ceiling is mild exasperation.

This is foolish, she thought but she dared not express her feelings aloud. She knew her father was concerned and she had no one to blame but herself.

I have been neglecting meals and sleeping poorly, she chided herself. *Now I have worried everyone.*

In minutes, she heard footfalls on the stairs and the door opened.

"*Guter mayire*, Kayla," Dr. Imhoff announced, smiling in his kindly way. "I understand you had a small fainting episode this morning."

Kayla stifled a sigh.

"It was nothing," she insisted.

"I will see about that," Jonah Imhoff replied lightly, opening his bag.

He checked her eyes and throat, running her temperature and pinching her skin to test for validity.

Then he turned to Jeremiah.

"We will talk outside," he told the patriarch, patting Kayla's face warmly.

"You should rest today, Kayla," he told her, closing his bag. Kayla chewed on her tongue to keep a thousand objections from erupting and watched helplessly as the men retreated into the hallway.

She strained her ears to listen, catching only a few words as she did.

"...tests...color...must be vigilant."

Their voices cut in and out but Kayla felt a prickle slide down her back as she understood the gist of their conversation.

He believes there is something wrong with me, she realized, concern floating through her for the first time since the incidents had begun. She tried to dismiss the feeling of worry but when her father returned to the bedroom, his eyes shone with something she had not seen in many years.

"Jonah is arranging for you to have tests done at Lancaster General Hospital," he told her gravely. Kayla swallowed quickly, realizing there was a lump in her throat.

"What does he believe is wrong, *Daed*?" she whispered and Jeremiah seemed to recognize his mistake, wiping the dismayed frown from his face.

"Nothing specific, *liebchen*," he replied quickly. "It is merely a precaution. Do not fret; we will learn what ails you soon enough."

"*Daed,* I am certain it is - "

"You are not a doctor, Kayla. In the meanwhile, you will rest. I will see if Lydia can stay with you while I tend to the farm," he continued and Kayla heard no room for debate in his tone.

"*Daed*, you cannot tend the farm alone," she sighed. "You would better have Lydia help you."

Jeremiah stared at her for a long while as if he was looking directly through her.

"You are correct," he told her softly. "I must enlist help until you are better."

Without another word, he spun and walked from the bedroom, leaving Kayla to stare after him with her mouth agape in question.

The wagon drew near the farmhouse, Lydia Fisher leading the horse through the grey day. They were returning from Kayla's appointment at the hospital where she had undergone bloodwork for her ever increasing fainting and general fatigue.

"Would you like me to come with you, Kayla?" Lydia asked as she slid from the bench onto the dirt. Kayla stifled a sigh and shook her head, forcing a smile onto her lips. She was growing tired of being coddled by both her father and the neighbors, despite their good intentions.

"I feel fine," she fibbed. In reality, she wished to lay down but she dared not say anything to Lydia. The last thing she wished to do was cause more of a fuss.

"I will be by later this evening to fix supper for you," Lydia told her, picking up the reins. "Back to bed now."

Kayla did not answer but waved at the butcher's wife as she made her way from the Roth farm toward her own.

I will go mad if I have to spend one more minute in bed, Kayla thought glumly, turning toward the fields. She saw her father in the distance, reaping corn and she longed to run toward him but she did not. She would only interrupt him and take more time from his duties.

Duties I should be tending to also, she told herself, guilt wracking her body.

The doctor at the hospital had been candid with her assessment, citing several reasons for her strange illness.

"But we will run the necessary tests, Kayla and determine the cause."

It was not until Kayla and Lydia were almost home that she realized that the physician had told her nothing of sustenance.

I can only wait for the results – however long that will take. In the meanwhile, Daed is working alone on the farm.

Suddenly, another figure appeared, close to the entrance of the maize and Kayla started.

"Hello!" she called out, her brow furrowing with concern. The stranger turned to look at her and he seemed to freeze as they stared at one another.

"Hello," he replied, turning to face her. Kayla stepped back in surprise as he emerged from the stalks, dressed in pair of blue jeans and a black and red flannel shirt.

"Who are you?" she demanded as she stared at him uncomprehendingly. "Does my father know you are here?"

The dark-haired man paused, cocking his head to the side slightly, a single strand of hair falling directly onto his forehead.

"Yes," he answered. "My name is Will. Will Jenkins."

Kayla waited for him to elaborate on why he stood on their land but he did not speak. Slowly, she drew closer to him.

"Why are you on our land?" Kayla asked, her green eyes narrowing in suspicion. She loathed that she was immediately concerned about the Englisher's presence but she could not reconcile one good reason that the man would be on the property.

"I am helping with the harvest," Will told her simply.

"Helping whom?"

Will stared at her for a long moment as if he was concerned she was slow-witted.

"I am helping the owner of the land obviously," he replied dryly. "Who are you?"

Kayla was reluctant to disclose any information to the man, her eyes lifting to see where her father was in the field.

Daed wouldn't hire an Englisher to help on the farm, she thought, distrustful of Will Jenkins. *And he certainly did not mention bringing on any help.*

To her relief, she was Jeremiah approaching.

"There is my father now," Kayla said sternly. "If you do not belong here, you best run along before he catches you on our property."

Will gave her a bemused smile.

"If I ran along, I would not be doing my job," he told her lightly. "I think your father would be angrier at that."

"Kayla you are home," Jeremiah cried, hurrying toward his daughter. She watched as he glanced nervously at the stranger.

"Come inside and we will talk," the senior Roth said, without acknowledging the Englisher in their midst. Kayla opened her mouth to speak but the look in her father's eye silenced her.

"Yes, *Daed*," she agreed, turning to follow Jeremiah inside the house. Will remained in place, his mouth upturned and Kayla cast him one long look before entering the house.

"Daed, did you hire that Englisher to help with the harvest?" she asked dubiously.

"Yes, but that is unimportant. Tell me what the doctor said," Jeremiah told her, abruptly changing the conversation.

"But *Daed*, I will be fine soon. You did not need to hire anyone, especially not an outsider!" Kayla cried.

Jeremiah's mouth became a fine line and his eyes narrowed.

"I do not wish to discuss the Englisher," he told her flatly. "I asked you about the doctor. What was said and what tests were done?"

Kayla swallowed another question.

"She believes that it is a blood disorder of sorts but I will not know until the tests come back. Simple bloodwork was performed. I will return next week for the results."

Jeremiah's brow knitted and he nodded.

"What sort of blood disorder?"

Kayla shrugged.

"I do not know, Daed. She did not give me specifics. I can only wait to learn."

Jeremiah did not seem happy with her answer but Kayla had little else to give him.

"Go rest now, Kayla. I will come to you after the work is done."

"*Daed*, may I go for Hannah? I do not wish to spend one more minute in bed. Please?"

Jeremiah regarded her for a long moment before bobbing his head reluctantly.

"If you are certain you are not feeling ill, you may pick up your sister from school. But you must come straight back to bed. Understood?"

Gratefully, Kayla nodded and hurried toward the front door before he could change his mind.

It will be lovely to stretch my legs and inhale the fresh autumn air, she thought. She was beginning to feel as a caged rabbit.

As she walked toward the road, she found herself looking back at Will Jenkins. He was hard at work, paying her no mind but as she turned in the direction of the schoolhouse, Kayla thought she could feel eyes on her.

Who is this man and what is he doing here?

That evening, Lydia Fisher came as promised, preparing a delicious supper for the Roths before heading home to her own family.

"She is a blessing to us," Jeremiah commented when she left and they sat down to eat. Kayla scowled slightly.

"She really doesn't need be here quite so often, *Daed*," she told her father. "I can still work."

"Your health is paramount, Kayla. Lydia has four able sons to work their farm and can spare a hand until you are well."

"I am well!" Kayla grunted, trying to keep the frustration from her voice. Jeremiah shot her a warning look and Kayla clamped her mouth closed. Arguing would not prove fruitful.

"Tell me about the Englisher," Kayla said instead and Hannah's head jerked upward from her stew.

"What Englisher?" the little girl asked curiously. Jeremiah's scowl deepened and he shook his head almost imperceivably at his oldest daughter.

"I have already explained that Will is helping with the harvest. There is nothing else to tell."

"Where did you find him, *Daed*? You must admit that it is odd to bring an outsider here when there are many in the community whom you could call upon for help."

Jeremiah's blue eyes seemed to darken.

"I am the head of this house," he snapped. "I do not need to answer to you for my choices."

Kayla was stung by his tone and she bit her lower lip. It was unlike her father to speak crossly to her or Hannah.

Whatever silliness is happening with me is causing him stress, she determined, taking a spoonful of beef stew. *I must not give him more of a reason to worry.*

She did not mention Will again but she decided that she would speak to Will the next time she saw him and learn more about him.

Kayla had her chance the following day. Jeremiah went to sell their goods at market, leaving Kayla alone.

"I have asked Lydia to come later in the day to ensure you are well," her father told her. Kayla rolled her eyes where he could not see.

You must not get annoyed, she warned herself but she could not help but feel frustrated at being treated like a child. She knew that was not Jeremiah's intention but she could not release the slight resentment she was feeling.

Her mother had died when she was fourteen, leaving Kayla as the woman of the household. Hannah was still an infant and Kayla had learned to tend to both the baby and the farm.

Standing idle was not something which she did well and she wished desperately that the doctors would quickly diagnose her issue so she was able to resume her role in the family and on the farm.

"Thank you, *Daed,*" she said instead of unleashing the barrage of protests vying to spring from her lips.

"I do not want you to leave the house today, Kayla," Jeremiah told her seriously as he stood in the doorway of her bedroom. "Stay inside and preferably in bed. If you are to faint with no one nearby..."

"I will not faint!" she cried but Jeremiah shook his head.

"You have no way of assuring me of that," he replied. "Please heed my words, Kayla. I speak only out of concern for you."

Begrudgingly, Kayla nodded.

"Yes, *Daed,*" she agreed. "I will take Hannah to school and – "

"No," Jeremiah said sharply. "Lydia will take your sister to school."

Kayla gritted her teeth and nodded.

"Have a good day in town, *Daed,*" Kayla sighed. She watched as he retreated to the freshly loaded wagon and disappeared down the road.

I have become a prisoner in my own home, Kayla thought mournfully, folding her arms across her chest. She wondered what she would do for the remainder of the day and as she thought it, she watched a silver sedan car driving up the road which Jeremiah had just taken.

Kayla leaned forward, watching the dilapidated vehicle pull onto their land, her pulse quickening. As she peered at the driver, she realized it was Will Jenkins arriving to work.

Is he supposed to be here today? She wondered nervously. If so, why hadn't her father told her to expect him.

Will jumped from the driver's seat and she noted he was wearing the same clothes he had the day before. He did not seem to notice her observing him, pulling a few items which she could not see from the backseat before turning toward the barn.

As Kayla rose her hand to wave in greeting, something tugged on her skirt.

"Kayla, I am hungry!" Hannah announced from behind her, causing the older girl to jump.

"You startled me, Hannah!" she chided and Hannah shrugged indifferently. She turned to usher her sister into the house, eyeing Will who had vanished behind the house.

I wonder if I should tend to him, she thought but her father's words reverberated in her mind.

"I do not want you to leave the house today, Kayla. Stay inside and preferably in bed. If you are to faint with no one nearby..."

She pushed the thought of Will Jenkins from her mind and closed the door.

She had no reason to approach the Englisher.

The weather had turned unseasonably warm and Kayla lifted her head from her book, realizing that the front room had grown almost stifling hot.

She cast the novel aside and reached to open the window, gazing into the fields. To her surprise, she saw Will Jenkins standing near the maple tree beside his car, wiping sweat from his brow.

Kayla watched him for a moment and she could see the sun and hard work had turned his face red.

He must be thirsty. He is dressed much too warmly to work the fields in that attire, she realized, rising from window seat.

A cool glass of water in hand, Kayla stepped into the yard. Will's back was to her and she tried to make herself heard as to not surprise him.

He turned and Kayla was filled with a strange sense of familiarity suddenly, something she had not felt the previous afternoon.

"Hello," he said and Kayla nodded, handing him the glass of water.

"It is very hot today," she volunteered. "I thought you might be thirsty."

He nodded gratefully and accepted the beverage, drinking it in one long gulp.

"I will fetch you another one," she offered and he shook his head.

"No, thank you," he replied. "I should be getting back to work."

He was older than Kayla with dark hair and vivid green eyes. His face seemed it had not been shaved in four days and there were dark circles under his eyes.

He is handsome in a rugged sort of way, she thought, studying his face. The feeling that she knew him did not diminish.

"As you wish," she replied, turning back.

"Actually wait," Will called nervously. He peered at his gloved hands in embarrassment as Kayla turned back to him.

"Yes?"

"Maybe one more glass of water," he muttered and Kayla smiled.

"Of course."

Inside the house, she thought of the somewhat bedraggled man on her lawn and she again wondered where he had come from.

If he has no water, he likely has no food either, she realized and quickly went to work preparing him a snack. *If he doesn't eat, he will also faint. Daed doesn't need to come home to such a sight.*

She did not want to think what her father would say if he knew she was feeding the Englisher.

Outside, she gestured for him to sit and eat. The gratitude in his face was beyond anything she had ever seen and a mixture of sadness and pity overwhelmed her.

"Are you from Lancaster, Mr. Jenkins?" Kayla asked timidly as he inhaled the bread and cheese she had brought to him. He shook his head and she waited for him to swallow the morsels before answering.

"No," he replied. "I am from Reading."

Kayla's brow furrowed.

"Reading?" she asked in surprise. "You have a little bit of a journey to make here."

Will nodded and shrugged his shoulders.

"It is an hour's drive," he answered. "But your father offered me very good pay and gas money for the trip."

None of what he said made sense to Kayla.

Why would Daed bring an Englisher to the district from an hour away?

"You know, I don't even know your name," Will commented as he polished off the last of the light meal she provided for him.

Embarrassed, Kayla extended her hand.

"Kayla Roth."

Will accepted her outstretched palm and they two looked at one another for a long moment. Kayla felt a sudden confusion as she stared at him.

Why do I feel such an affinity with this man? She wondered, an almost awe-struck feeling overcoming her.

"Nice to meet you, Kayla. I should be getting back to work. I don't want your dad to think he's wasting his money."

Kayla stepped back reluctantly, wanting to speak with him longer but she knew he was right. There was much work to be done and she had detained the harvest enough already.

"If you should need more water, Mr. Jenkins," Kayla told him. "There is a spigot beside the barn."

He looked at her thankfully.

"You truly are a lifesaver, Miss Roth. You and your father have helped me a great deal already."

Kayla did not know how to respond but Will did not seem to require an answer.

She slipped back into the house and reclaimed her window seat but her book was forgotten. She spent the remainder of the afternoon watching Will working in the field and wondering if *Gotte* had sent him to their farm for a reason.

Kayla waited impatiently for her father to take Hannah to school before hurrying outside to greet Will who was cleaning the stalls. Her father would not be gone long but she wanted to talk to the man again, if only for a short time.

"Good morning, Miss Roth," Will said brightly. She smiled.

"You may call me Kayla," she told him. "I brought you muffins if you are hungry."

She offered them to him and he took them happily. For the third day, he donned the same clothes and Kayla wondered if he had any other garments.

He is obviously not well off. I wonder if that is why Daed brought him here; to help a man down on his luck.

"In that case, you can call me Will," he laughed, taking a bite of the muffin in his hand. His dark eyebrows shot up.

"This is great!" he said. "Did you make this yourself?"

She nodded.

"The Amish can do everything," he sighed. "I knew an Amish girl once. She never failed to amaze me with her talents."

"What happened to her?" Kayla asked curiously, leaning against a stall door. Will smiled thinly.

"She returned to her community. Decided the outside world wasn't for her after all."

Kayla could read the regret in his face but before she could ask anything else, she felt herself grow lightheaded.

Oh no! She thought as bright lights colored her line of sight.

"Kayla?" Will's voice sounded very far away and suddenly she was in his arms as her legs buckled beneath her. She willed herself to take deep breaths and to her relief she did not faint.

"Are you all right?" Will demanded as she regained her footing. Slowly he released her and Kayla stood on shaking legs.

She nodded, shifting her eyes downward.

"I get fainting spells sometimes," she confessed as the spots cleared from her vision. Will's emerald eyes narrowed.

"Have you been to the doctor?" he asked and Kayla bobbed her head.

"I am awaiting test results," she told him, sighing. "They believe it is some sort of blood disorder."

Will's mouth became a tight, white line.

"Is that so?" he asked quietly.

"Kayla! What are you doing in here?" Jeremiah appeared in the doorway, his face pale as he took in the scene before him.

"I – I came to offer Mr. Jenkins some muffins," she murmured, averting her eyes from his shocked face.

"You should not be in here," he told his daughter, shooing her from the barn.

"Thank you for the muffins, Kayla," Will called after her. "I hope you are feeling better."

Jeremiah led the way back to the house and did not say a word until they were inside, whirling to confront Kayla.

"Why were you speaking with Will Jenkins?" he demanded furiously. "I told you that you are to stay in the house."

"Daed, I am growing mad staying in the house!" Kayla protested. "And Will seems a very nice man!"

Jeremiah's expression was indecipherable as he stared at his oldest daughter. He seemed to be considering his next words carefully.

"You are to stay away from Will Jenkins," he told her firmly. "I do not want you anywhere near him, do you understand?"

Kayla's eyebrows knit together.

"No," she answered truthfully. "Of course I do not understand. Why would you ask me to stay away from him?"

"He is not someone whom you should associate yourself," Jeremiah insisted. Kayla stared at him uncomprehendingly.

"*Daed*, if he is such a terrible man, why would you have him come to our home?"

"He not in our home. He is merely helping with harvest. I want you to swear that you will not have any further contact with him. Swear it, Kayla!"

Kayla did not know what to say. She wanted to promise her father that she wouldn't see the Englisher again but she knew her curiosity would not keep her away.

"Kayla!"

She hung her head and nodded, sighing deeply.

"I swear it, *Daed*," she breathed but she wondered if she would be able to honor her oath.

Kayla did not risk going to Will until the next time her father went to the market, three days later. She found herself watching the worker from the window often, willing him to take notice of her and sometimes he would lift his head and acknowledge her with a half-wave but never in Jeremiah's presence.

This makes little sense. Daed brings him from out of town to work and then speaks as if the man is a danger to us.

The previous day, she had gone to the hospital for her test results.

"As we suspected, Kayla, you have a blood disorder called megaloblastic anemia. It can be treated with supplements and dietary changes but it is manageable," the doctor informed her. Kayla nodded, relieved the diagnosis was simple.

"When will I be able to resume my work?" she asked eagerly and the doctor chuckled.

"We will start your injections immediately and you should notice a change within a week or so. The fatigue and dizziness will lessen and you will be back to normal in no time."

Kayla peered at the physician.

"What causes this?" she asked with interest.

"In your case, it is genetic," the doctor replied.

After Hannah left for school and her father for the market, Kayla rushed outside to speak with Will.

"Kayla, you should not be out here," he told her, his jaw locking when she appeared. Kayla was hurt by his words.

"I do not understand; why does my father wish to keep me away from you?" she asked bluntly but Will did not answer as he continued to bale hay.

"I'm sorry," she muttered, turning away. "I only came to tell you that I got my results from the hospital. I have a blood disorder – anemia."

Will's head jerked up to stare at her, his mouth open slightly.

"What kind of anemia?" he demanded. Kayla wracked her mind to recall the proper term.

"Mega...mega..."

"Megaloblastic?"

Kayla smiled.

"Yes, that is it."

Kayla waited for him to return her grin but his face went dark.

"You should go back in the house. You don't want your father to catch you out here."

She stared at him, tears of humiliation filling her eyes.

I thought we had a bond, she thought miserably, chewing on her lower lip.

"Hurry up," Will growled, pointing at the house. Kayla spun, tears spilling down her cheeks as she ran back inside.

Daed was right; I should have just stayed away from him.

"Kayla! *Daed* is yelling!" Hannah cried, flying into the kitchen where Kayla was doing the dishes.

"What?"

"He is yelling at the Englisher!" Hannah insisted, pointing toward the front of the house. Kayla quickly dried her hands on her apron and rushed toward the door. As she pulled open the heavy wood, she heard a car door slam and watched as Will screeched away in his rundown sedan.

Jeremiah stood, his arms folded angrily across his chest as he watched the man leave and Kayla was sure she had never seen him look so intimidating.

"*Daed*! *Daed,* what happened?" she cried, rushing toward him. He whirled to face her, his face undergoing several expressions, settling on near-panic.

"Nothing," he replied gruffly. "Go inside."

"*Daed* please!" she begged. "What happened with Will?"

His eyes narrowed dangerously and he shook his head.

"I made a mistake bringing him here," he muttered, storming toward the house. "Do not mention his name in this house again."

Bewildered, Kayla turned toward the road but of course Will was long gone.

She looked helplessly at her father but she was only staring at his retreating back and Kayla was filled with an inexplicable sense of loss.

He is not coming back, she realized and the thought made her sick to her stomach for reasons she could not comprehend.

Life on the Roth farm returned to normal and as promised, Kayla began to feel better as the treatments took effect.

The harvest went well and Will Jenkins did not return to the district but his memory was fresh in Kayla's mind.

Perhaps one day, Daed will tell me who he was truly and how he came to be here. But she did not have high hopes for that occurring. Jeremiah never brought up the Englisher again and Kayla did not dare.

It was the beginning of November when the letter arrived.

It was slipped between the screen door and it had not been mailed.

Without opening it, Kayla suspected she knew who had written it but as she tore into the envelope, her suspicions were confirmed.

Her hands trembling, she read the letter, her heart thumping wildly.

Dear Kayla, it read. *I have wrestled with whether to write this letter or leave well enough alone as your father wanted. I can't live my life without telling you who I am because I think you deserve the truth. As you know, my name is William Jenkins. Twenty years ago, I met a beautiful girl in Lancaster and we fell madly in love. I mentioned that I once knew an Amish girl and that girl was your mother, Anna. We had plans to marry but one day, I woke up and she was gone. She had left me a letter, much like the one I am writing you, apologizing for her choice and claiming she had made a mistake leaving her community. She begged me not to look for her and I agreed. I left town and moved to Reading, not wanting to run into her. If I had stayed, I would have learned that she married Jeremiah Roth and soon gave birth to a beautiful baby daughter; you.*

If I had not seen your eyes, I may never have known that you were mine but there is no mistaking you are my child.

I did not understand why your father had brought me to your farm until I heard you were sick. Megaloblastic anemia is genetic – I know because I have it also. I suspect Jeremiah was terribly concerned for your health and wanted to learn about your family history. I don't think he ever intended for us to meet and when we did and I learned the truth, he grew angry and banished me from the farm. I want you to know that if I had known you were my child, I would have always been in your life.

You may do what you wish with this information, Kayla. You may choose to never see me again or you may confront your father. Shamefully I do not know you well enough to know how you will react but I would like to get to know you. You are a grown woman and I can't force a relationship on you.

Whatever you do, please remember that your father only did what he did to keep you safe, happy and healthy. If you decide to let him know that you know, go easy on him. He is the only father you have ever had after all.

I have enclosed my phone number and mailing address. I will not hold my breath but I will hold onto hope that you will see me again.

Whatever you choose, know that I support you and love you. I wish you only the best this world has to offer.

Love always,

Will

Tears flowed freely down Kayla's face and the words grew blurry as she read and re-read the letter, her breath escaping in shuddering sobs.

"Oh Gotte, Kayla!" Jeremiah cried, entering the foyer where his oldest daughter stood. "What happened?"

Kayla shook her head and stuffed the letter back into the envelope, wiping her face with the back of her hand.

"Nothing, nothing," she gasped. He stared at her, his face a mask of worry and Kayla had never been filled with so much love for another person.

Does he know I know? Has he been filled with worry for the past nineteen years that the truth would come out and he would lose the daughter he had raised as his own? Kayla could not imagine the pain her father must have endured over the years.

He is the only father I have ever known. He is my Daed no matter what that letter reads.

Impulsively, she threw herself into her father's arm, burying her face in his broad chest.

"I love you, *Daed*," she whispered, inhaling the comforting scent of his dirty work clothes.

"I love you, daughter," he sighed.

In that moment, Kayla knew she would honor her father's wishes and never again bring up Will Jenkin's name in their home.

That did not mean she would never see the Englisher again.

END

SMALL TOWN CHURCH ROMANCE

CHELSEA BECKS

"YOU WILL GO TO HELL. THE POWER OF CHRIST COMPELS YOU. THE POWER OF CHRIST WILL SAVE YOU IF YOU BELIEVE IN HIM. THE POWER OF CHRIST WILL KEEP YOU FROM HELL. GET YOUR ACT TOGETHER AND BELIEVE IN GOD."

Sara was a little freaked out.

Okay . . . Sara was really freaked out.

"So my cousin is a pharmacist and she can totally sneak me some Valium for this guy," Miranda, next to her, whispered in her ear.

Sara only went to church because it was routine. That wasn't to say she wasn't a pretty good Christian; she never killed anybody and she didn't eat meat on Fridays. Sometimes she prayed before she went to bed, and she never said the Lord's name in vain. Well. She tried not to.

"Look at that vein that bulges in his neck," Sara whispered to Miranda.

"Watch it burst," Miranda said smugly.

Sara tried not to smile.

No one in the congregation was okay with Pastor Henry being a total freak show. In fact it was completely surprising that their old pastor, Pastor Samuel, had picked him for his replacement at all. The young guy was new in town, and seemed to be totally normal, but how did he pass the job interview? Sara imagined Pastor Samuel in Boca or wherever he was, having a good laugh about his little practical joke, before informing all of them that the real Pastor would start next Sunday.

"He's kind of cute," Callie, from the other side of Miranda, said.

"Gross," Sara and Miranda said in unison.

Pastor Henry didn't hear any of this. "DO YOU THINK WHAT YOU ARE DOING IS OKAY? DO YOU REALIZE JESUS DIED FOR ALL OF YOU AND ALL YOU DO IS DISOBEY THE WORD OF GOD. REAL CLASSY. REALLY REALLY CLASSY. JUST YOU WAIT. JUST YOU WAIT FOR THE GLORIOUS

DAYS OF REVELATION! YOU KNOW THE RIVER? THE TOWN RIVER? I WANT YOU ALL THERE TOMORROW AT SUNSET! THERE I WILL REPENT YOU OF YOUR SINS AND YOU WON'T ROT IN HELL LIKE YOU SHOULD!"

"Pop," Miranda whispered.

"TO QUOTE REVELATION:
BUT THE FEARFUL, AND UNBELIEVING, AND THE ABOMINABLE, AND MURDERERS, AND WHORE MONGERS, AND SORCERERS, AND IDOLATERS, AND ALL LIARS, SHALL HAVE THEIR PART IN THE LAKE WHICH BURNETH WITH FIRE AND BRIMSTONE: WHICH IS THE SECOND DEATH!

AVOID THE SECOND DEATH MY PARISHIONERS. AVOID THE SECOND DEATH AND FIND JESUS IN YOUR HEART. MEET ME AT THE RIVER AT SUNSET. THE RIVER AT SUNSET. BE THERE OR ROT IN HELL!"

After church, everyone usually met in the hall for coffee hour. The girls did as not to say no to free food, but they noticed the crowd was a little thinner than usual.

"I wonder if he's gonna keep screaming?" Miranda asked, helping herself to a donut.

"It was kind of hot," Callie said.

"You're weird. You two deserve each other in hell."

The girls were then interrupted by the presence of Miss Hattie: the church clerk who was as wide as she was tall . . . and she was pretty tall. She plowed right between the group and helped herself to two donuts. "Hey, girls!" she said, the natural volume of her voice set to "loud". Her church dress that she wore every week was a dusty rose color with bright blue flowers and purple polka dots, her gray hair set in curls around her face.

"Hey, Miss Hattie," the three said in unison.

"Isn't it nice that even though your parents are dead all you girls still come to church?" She smiled brightly.

"Our parents aren't dead," Callie said, acknowledging herself and Sara.

"And my parents have been dead my whole life." Miranda had lived with her aunt and uncle since she was a baby.

"Oh." It was clear that Miss Hattie's memory was evading her, but she would never admit it. She smiled, and the girls noticed a streak of lipstick on her front teeth. "Well, anyway, we like to see young folk in the congregation."

"Is that why Pastor Samuel appointed a young minister?" Sara wondered. If anyone was going to spill the details on the parish's opinion of Pastor Henry it was going to be Miss Hattie.

Miss Hattie pursed her lips. "Well, now, you see I told Pastor Samuel that appointing a woman wouldn't be a bad idea. You know Rose Becker? Her daughter Lucy has just gotten her license or whatever they call it and she's a wonderful preacher, has a presence, and she's not too pretty so following the word of God might be able to find her someone. Anyway, I suggested to Pastor Samuel to appoint Lucy, and did he listen to me? Nope! He just appointed Henry, and I gotta say girls, he's a bit too aggressive for my liking."

The girls nodded in agreement, and Sara was grateful Callie didn't mention how cute she thought he was.

Before the conversation could progress, Pastor Henry was next to them. Close up, Sara noticed he wasn't a bad looking guy. He had dusty blonde hair, brown eyes, and nice features. He didn't look the least bit scary at all up close. He didn't even having the vein popping out of his neck.

"Hello," he said. Even his voice was quiet. "I'm just trying to go around and meet everyone."

"Well, you already met me," Miss Hattie said, clearly offended.

"Yes, Miss Hattie, I have met you." He even smiled, and Sara noticed it was a nice smile. "And you are all . . ?

"Calliope Calavant," Callie said. She completely made that up. Her real name was Callie Smith, but whenever she was meeting a new guy she liked to sound exotic.

"Miranda," Miranda said. "I don't have a last name."

Sara decided that since they were in a church she should be honest. "Sara Clevenger," she said. "Nice to meet you."

"Nice to meet all of you." Henry nodded. "I hope to see you all at the river tomorrow night. It really will be a fun time."

"Can you promise that?" Callie asked. The other two rolled their eyes.

"Yes," he laughed, but Sara noticed that Henry was looking at her when he said it. "I can promise that."

The girls went to brunch like they usually did on Sundays, and then Sara rushed home. Her mother had just left for work, picking up an extra shift at the bar she worked at, which meant her father was alone. He couldn't be that way for too long.

"Hey dad," Sarah said. Her father, Bill, was sitting in the recliner watching TV, his wheelchair next to him. He was dressed in his usual sweatpants and black T-shirt, his mouth open slightly as he looked at his daughter. He smiled. "Did you eat lunch yet?"

Bill managed a little nod. He couldn't speak. He had ALS, a diagnoses that tore Sara's family apart emotionally, but they still managed to stay together. Sara moved back home while her mother worked more to help take care of her dad.

"Are you comfy?" Sara asked, but then proceeded to fluff the pillow behind his back a little more. She looked at the TV. He was watching the baseball game, so at least he was actually entertained and not faking it for the amusement of his wife.

"Are you OK?" Sara asked.

Bill looked at her, and nodded. Sara couldn't help but smile at her father. "Okay," she said.

Henry lived in the rectory next to the church. He never had to pay rent and it was well lined so it was never too cold. He liked making a fire and drank tea every night while doing his Bible readings.

As he read that night, his mind flicked back to church. He knew his methods were extreme, but his favorite pastor had the same approach and where he grew up everyone loved the way that he preached. He wasn't sure how the new church felt about it, however. They all looked a little scared.

He then thought about Sara. The other two girls she was with were pretty, but there was something about her that really stood out to him. Maybe because she didn't have that pinched look on her face like Miranda, or because she didn't immediately try to jump in his pants like Callie. She was calm, and polite, and . . . beautiful.

He wasn't too sure about the meeting at the river the next day, but he was positive that she would show up. She did look interested when he mentioned it . . . unless he totally imagined that she did.

Henry looked out the window, wrapping his fingers around his warm tea cup and watched as the sun began to set. His street had the most perfect view of the horizon. He wondered if Sara liked sunsets.

Henry shook his head, and hoped that she would show up to the river. He hoped that she would like it. He hoped the whole town would.

That night, after Sara had put Bill to bed, her mother Nancy came home, finding Sara in the kitchen doing dishes. Nancy was a woman that aged too quickly. Having a dying spouse would do that to you. She was still pretty though, with blonde hair like her only daughter, and blue eyes. She worked hard at the bar, and made pretty good money. She needed to to take care of Bill.

"Hungry?" Sara asked. "I made Dad scrambled eggs. I could whip you up some."

Nancy collapsed at the table and shook her head. "I ate at work. How did he do?"

Sara bit her lip. "He didn't eat much. He tried to, but I don't think he was that hungry."

Nancy nodded, not bothering to hide how unbelievable exhausted she was. "How was church? The new preacher started today, didn't he?

"He wants to dunk us all in the river to repent us of our sins," Sara said, dropping the plate she was holding as the water suddenly got really hot. She turned down the dial and braved to pick it up again. "He's pretty crazy. He screamed the entire time instead of just giving a normal sermon. It was really uncomfortable."

"He probably just doesn't understand the way we are used to things." Nancy always tried to sympathize with things that were generally not well liked. Her favorite animal was the opossum.

"Or he's crazy," Sara laughed.

"I want you to go to that river dunk thing tomorrow," Nancy said. "Just give it a try. It's important we support members of the community. That church has helped us out so much since your father got sick, it's the least you could do."

Sara didn't want to argue with her mother. She didn't want to go, but she knew that if it was important to Nancy than it should be important to her. She decided not to ask Miranda and Callie if they were going too. She didn't want to get laughed at.

At seven o'clock the next evening, Henry waited by the river. It was the main water source in town, leading right into the reservoir. He figured the river would be a good place for the re-baptism of the congregation. He loved water. He loved its healing spirit. He hoped everyone else would too .No one was there yet, but he realized that "sunset" was a bit of a vague time. Maybe everyone else did not read the same solar clock he did and would be there in a little bit. He checked his watch. 7:01.

At quarter after, he checked his watch for the umpteenth time. No one was there yet. Henry could feel his smile begin to fade.

7:30, the sun was beginning to be a peachy color, and night was beginning to overtake the sky when he heard the car pull up. It parked on the grass, and the driver got out. It took him a second to realize it was Sara, and suddenly it did not matter that no one else in the congregation had showed up to the baptism.

"Pastor Henry," she said.

"It's just Henry."

She nodded. "Henry."

"Sara."

"Are you going to scream at me while you dunk me in the river, or is it completely okay if I just go about and do this myself?"

He felt a little uneasy. "I can give you a blessing," he said. "And I promise I won't scream."

She took off her shirt, and while the motion caught him off guard, Henry realized that she was wearing a one piece bathing suit. She stripped off her jean, and stood on the grass, curling it under her toes. He then took off his pants to his swim suit, and hesitated about his shirt, before realizing that it really didn't matter, then took it off. He was happy that for the first time in his life he was actually in somewhat good of shape, then realized how wrong it was of him to be thinking like that when he was about to baptize someone.

Him and Sara walked toward the river. He dunked his foot in, and realized the water was just a little bit warmer than ice. This would be quick. Sara, meanwhile, did not hesitate. She plunged right in, under the water, the light current not swaying her a bit. She resurfaced, and slicked her wet hair off her face with her hands before smiling. "Was that too premature for a blessing?" she asked.

"No," Henry replied, awing at how beautiful she looked in the sunset.

"It's better just to go right in," she explained. "Otherwise you'll be shivering. This way your body gets used to it."

Henry supposed she was right. He hadn't swam since summer camp when he was a kid; and even then he barely ever did. He was too busy reading a book to socialize with the other kids. Henry had never been much of a people person, even as a child. He turned to the church and his faith and the pastor who taught him so much, and only then was he able to find any comfort in himself.

Henry decided to just go for it, and dove right into the icy water, feeling it seep through his skin and freeze his veins. When he came up for air, he gasped, and then registered that Sara was laughing at him. He stood up, and shook his hair, before saying, "How the hell did you do that?"

"Did you just say hell?" she mused.

"I'm human, you know," he muttered.

Sara grinned. "Okay, so this baptism or whatever . . . let's just do this."

Henry nodded, then waded through the water so that he was standing right next to Sara. "I do this for you. I do this for your soul."

She nodded, and maybe he was imagining it, but she seemed to be staring at him.

"I'm going to dip your head in the water now."

She was treading in the shallow water, and he held her forehead as she dipped her hair under the water. He tried not to run his fingers through her hair. He tried to be professional, as he recited:

Living and Loving Father,

I praise and thank You with my heart for the liberation You have given me from the clutches of sin and Satan. By Your death on the Cross of Calvary, You have put my old life with its sin and judgment to death forever, and endowed me with a new life that is abounding with joy. Father, I commit this Baptism Day into Your most precious and loving hands. I believe that by Your crucifixion on the Cross, my old self was rendered powerless and I was freed from all sin. You were raised from the dead that I too may live a life victorious and overcoming all evil. Father, this day, I rededicate myself to live in You and live a life for Your glory. I remember the day when I was baptized and washed off all my sins. Lord, it is Your grace that I must be counted worthy to be called Your child. Help me to keep Your commandments. Renew my strength this day that I may be strong in faith and increase in zeal. Preserve me for the glorious day of Your coming. I believe Your Word which says, "He who has begun a good work in you will complete it until the day of Jesus Christ." Let this day be the beginning. Lead me into greater spiritual depths even in the coming days. In Jesus' precious name I pray.

Amen.

Henry traced the cross on her forehead with his thumb. "Amen," he whispered again, and then gently helped Sara lift her head up.

They locked eyes for a second, and that was when Henry noticed his hand was around her waist. Sara noticed too, but she did not try to stop it, in fact she felt like it should be there.

"So I'm not going to hell?" she whispered.

"No way," he whispered back.

Before he could acknowledge that it was happening, he was kissing her, or was she kissing him? They were kissing each other, and behind them the sun officially set.

The darkness over came the river, and noticing that their visibility was waning, Sara and Henry stopped before getting out of the river. Henry did not know what to say to her, other than a slew of apologies that was normal for him to spurt out in this type of situation. However, instead, he noticed she was smiling and said, "Was that okay?"

Sara laughed. "That was fine."

She realized she didn't bring a towel, so she put her clothes on over her soaking wet bathing suit. Henry put on his shirt, and then felt a little awkward about the situation. Even though kissing Sara was better than he imagined, he realized then he really did not know her at all, and to her he was just the screaming preacher.

"I'm sorry." His familiar words came out of his mouth.

"I kissed you," she said, giving him a weird look.

"I thought I kissed you?"

They were quiet for a second, and then both laughed.

Sara didn't expect any of that to happen, except for maybe the fact that she would be the only one to show up for the baptism ritual by the river. Flushed, and feeling happy for whatever reason, she went home to shower, and then proceeded to get ready for a night out with Callie and Miranda.

They all met at their favorite restaurant outside of town, where on Mondays the cocktails were half price after nine. Miranda wore a low cut sweater, and Callie an even tighter one. Sara tried not to smile to broadly when she sat down at the table.

"Who did you lay?" Callie asked.

"No one," Sara muttered, taking a sip of the martini her friends had already ordered her. She knew how the others felt about Henry, and since she didn't know if she really liked him yet she figured she should maybe keep the events of the evening to herself.

"Boring." Miranda rolled her eyes.

They all ordered a variety of appetizers, and the conversation as usual took a turn to talking about hot men. A little tipsy, Sara tried her best to keep her mouth shut, but eventually she was dying with curiosity.

"Henry is pretty hot," she said.

"Pastor Henry?" Callie asked. "Hell yeah."

"Nope." Miranda winced and shook her head. "Absolutely not. Nuh uh. No way."

"I think I like him," Sara said, and then she slurped her martini instead of looking at her friends for their reactions. When she deemed enough time had passed, she dared a glance, and saw both of them with their mouths wide open, not unlike a fish above water.

"Don't do it!" Miranda warned.

"Don't!"

"Think of your father!"

"Think of the women and children!"

"He's CRAZY!"

"ABSOLUTELY insane!"

"Even Miss Hattie didn't like him!"

It was clear that Miranda and Callie were getting hysterical. Around them, other people in the restaurant began to stare, and Sara was getting more and more uncomfortable. She was not expecting this much of an outburst.

"Okay, okay!" Sara held her hand up to silence them. "Keep your pants on. I won't do anything about it."

Although her friends looked relieved, deep inside Sara felt a little hurt. She tried not to imagine kissing Henry for the rest of the reason, but she found it really hard not to.

Henry was sitting in his office the next day writing a sermon when he heard the knock on the door. "Come in," he said.

The door opened, and he didn't bother to look up, figuring it was just Miss Hattie, when a familiar and beautiful voice said, "We need to talk."

He looked up and saw Sara there. She was wearing a dress, her hair tied back, and even though she wasn't dripping wet in the sunset she was still beautiful. Henry thought she may be too good to be true. "Sara," he said. "Come in."

She did, which he took as a good sign. He was glad he cleaned off his desk that morning; he didn't want her thinking he was a slob. Sara sighed. "We have to talk . . . about your preaching."

"You don't like it?" he asked.

"You're a little . . . aggressive," Sara said, and then she bit her lip. "It's scaring all of your friends."

"You're scared of what your friends think?" Maybe Sara was one of those shallow girls that Henry had known growing up. He couldn't help but feel a pit of disappointment form in his stomach.

"My friends . . . the town . . ." Sara winced. "You're just so different from Pastor Samuel. He was gentle and sweet and at first I thought that maybe the aggressive and angry, brimstone and fire speech was just what you were, but after what happened at the river . . . you're a nice guy, Henry. You're kind and charming and the person who baptized me and the person who was screaming Revelation were not the same person."

"Pastor Samuel knew what he was hiring," Henry said, feeling a little angry. "He knew what my style was and he liked it and when I was hired . . . he knew what he was getting."

"We don't know if it was a joke though."

Sara regretted it the moment she said it. Henry, meanwhile, did not know her well enough to figure that out. He stood up and pointed to the door. "I think you should leave."

"Henry . . ."

"Now."

She stood up and made her way to the door. Before she left though, she turned around and said, "I really liked the kissing, by the way. I really like you."

And with that, she left, and Henry was more confused and hurt than ever.

Sara cried in the car on the way home, to get it out of her system before she saw her father and she had to be strong for him. She wiped her face, and reapplied her mascara, before going inside the house. Her father was sleeping in his wheelchair in the kitchen; the warmest room in the house because of the sunlight that swallowed the room through the big bay window.

She decided not to disturb him, and made herself a peanut butter and jelly sandwich. As she ate, she watched her father. His chest was rising and falling slowly; he was still breathing. She knew she only had months more with him, and dreaded the moment when his chest would no longer rise and fall and he would be nothing more than a memory. His disease was always fatal, and there was nothing she could do about it but enjoy the time she had left with him.

When she was done eating, Bill opened his eyes.

"Hey, Dad," she said.

He tried to smile.

"I think I might have done something stupid.

When her father was functional, the two were close. Now, however, since he could not spill all of her secrets to the world, Sara found herself telling him everything that was on her mind. Since he could smile and sometimes shake his head, it was a sort of effective way of communication. It made her feel better at least.

"I kissed the pastor."

Bill opened his eyes wider.

"Not Pastor Samuel. Pastor Henry. The new pastor. He's young, and kind, and super socially awkward . . . he's a really great guy. I can tell. But he's a yeller. He screams about Satan and he wanted to dunk everyone in the river to repent their sins and . . . no one likes him. No one. Not Miranda or Callie or Miss Hattie . . ."

Bill didn't say anything, or even react.

"I don't know what to do, Dad."

Suddenly, Sara thought her father was choking. He started making noise, and she ran over to him, but Bill tried to push her aside as best as he could. She stopped, and looked at her father, and his eyes widened a little more. "Give," he stammered. "Him. A Ch-ch-chance."

Sara teared up: her father hadn't spoken in over a month. "Dad?"

He coughed a little, and then swallowed, and nodded., then smiled.

"Give him a chance?"

Bill nodded.

If it had been any other person besides her father, who had used all of her strength to tell her that, she most likely would have ignored it. "Okay," Sara nodded, still teared up. "I will."

Henry thought a lot about what Sara had told him, and as much as he did not want to listen to a woman and do what she told him to do, he also had to take in account what was best for his congregation.

He arranged a meeting with Miss Hattie and, just like Sara had told him, she agreed that his sermons needed to die down a little bit. Henry called up Pastor Samuel, who said that hiring Henry was not a joke, but he hoped that he would learn his lesson and arrange his sermons to be friendlier. He also wished Henry luck with Sara, and hoped the best for him.

Henry spent the last few days of the week to write Sunday's sermon. He hoped Sara and the rest of the congregation would like it.

On Sunday, he dressed in his robes, and began the service. He spoke quietly, but not too quiet, and tried not to let his nerves get the best of him. He tried not to look at Sara too much, but there she was: sitting in the second row with her wretched friends, a small smile on her face the entire time.

Then, it was time for the sermon. Again, he spoke quietly, and firmly, and then when it was close to an end, he said, "I am new in town. I am a new preacher, and you are a new community. As many of you know Jesus was a stranger in many lands amongst his travels, and although his methods weren't as . . . extreme . . . as mine, he did get some ridicule. But there were also those that gave him a chance, and those who helped him become well known and lead him down the road for him to help him save us. I want us all to grow as a community and to become followers of Jesus and God together, so today, I propose that after service we all go down to the river and pray together, and wash away all of our sins and start a fresh. A new community. A new start. And now, I want to pray:

Great Redeemer and Father of all nations, I humbly come before your throne and offer my thanks and praise for all that you have done to bless us, your people. Please let me know you and be aware of your daily presence in my life. Forgive me, dear Father, when I haven't been a suitable place for your grace and name to dwell. Thank you for redeeming me from the sin that once entangled me. Guard my heart and rescue me from the deceptive lies of the evil one. In Jesus' name, and I say his prayer, Our father, who art in heaven, hallow by thy name, thy kingdom come, thy will be done, on earth as it in in heaven. Give us this day our daily bread, and forgive our trespasses, as we forgive those who trespass against us, and lead us not into temptation, but deliver us from evil, for thine is the kingdom and the power and the glory forever. Amen.

"Amen," the congregation echoed after him. When Henry lifted his head from prayer, he saw Sara smile at him.

After church, Henry skipped the coffee hour, and went right to the river. He did not expect anyone to come, but he figured maybe it would be okay. He had prayer and, he hoped, he had Sara.

She showed up first, a couple minutes after he did. She brought a blanket. They laid it on the grass and sat next to each other, finding calm in watching the river gently roll by. They didn't talk for a moment, but then Henry realized she was holding his hand.

"A week ago, I never would have expected this," Sara finally said.

"Me either."

"A week ago, I never thought that I would be falling in love with you."

Henry looked at her, and the two of them locked eyes. She smiled, and he felt like he could kiss her, but then the sound of a car came, pulling up. He didn't know the names of the people coming towards them, but he knew they were members of the church. He stood up, breaking away from Sara, to greet them. When he extended his hand they took it, and that was a good sign.

Soon, more and more people showed up. Some brought food. One brought a portable grill. It wasn't the type of baptism Henry was expecting, but he found himself helping the guy set it up and helped make burgers for everyone. A few kids brought frisbies. Some people swam in the river. Miranda and Callie even showed up and, although Miranda's stare was still uncomfortable, Henry took it as a good sign that she was there.

Eventually, after everyone had eaten, Henry took them all into the river. He instructed everyone to get into pairs, and they would do this twice, each time one person holding their partner up as he read them the prayer of baptism and helped them wash away all of their sins. The entire congregation of roughly 100 people paired up and waded into the river, and he blessed them with the same prayer he blessed Sara:

Living and Loving Father,

I praise and thank You with my heart for the liberation You have given me from the clutches of sin and Satan. By Your death on the Cross of Calvary, You have put my old life with its sin and judgment to death forever, and endowed me with a new life that is abounding with joy. Father, I commit this Baptism Day into Your most precious and loving hands. I believe that by Your crucifixion on the Cross, my old self was rendered powerless and I was freed from all sin. You were raised from the dead that I too may live a life victorious and overcoming all evil. Father, this day, I rededicate myself to live in You and live a life for Your glory. I remember the day when I was baptized and washed off all my sins. Lord, it is Your grace that I must be counted worthy to be called Your child. Help me to keep Your commandments. Renew my strength this day that I may be strong in faith and increase in zeal. Preserve me for the glorious day of Your coming. I believe Your Word which says, "He who has begun a good work in you will complete it until the day of Jesus Christ." Let this day be the beginning. Lead me into greater spiritual depths even in the coming days. In Jesus' precious name I pray.

Amen.

At the end, most of the people continued swimming when Sara noticed another car pulling up, squeezing in between two other cars that had unevenly parked on the grass. She thought . . . but it couldn't be.

Nancy was pushing Bill toward the river before she knew it, and Sara couldn't help but smile. Her father had not left his house in a long time, and it was truly a miracle that he was strong enough to be able to at all.

"Henry," Sara said to him. "I want you to meet my father."

The two walked toward Bill. Sara introduced Henry to her parents, and Bill smiled at the pastor. "You have a beautiful daughter," Henry told him.

Bill smiled wider.

"And honestly . . ." Henry blushed a little. "I think I'm falling in love with her."

Bill struggled, but a moment later, he was able to lift his hand enough for Henry to grab it. The two men shook hands, and around then a congregation celebrated becoming even closer together.

AMBER & ABEL

MONICA MARKS

Amber and Abel

Milan, Italy

"No! No! No!" Amber cried, throwing her hands up in dismay. "How did this happen? How *could* this happen?"

The others in the hung their heads in unison, no one willing to accept the blame for the most recent catastrophe.

"Giuliana is to wear the taffeta number, Gia the silk and Corina the leather and lace. Who screwed this up? Come on, speak up. Time is money, people!"

Again, only mollified silence met the designer's question.

Amber stifled a groan, knowing that she would not get an admission from the group.

"Never mind now," she sighed. "Twenty minutes to curtain. Get the models re-dressed at once. Keep an eye on the rotation! It's simple reading! It's not that complicated!"

A chorus of "yes ma'am" filled her ears and she spun to deal with the next mishap as someone shoved a clipboard in her face.

It doesn't matter how many years I've been doing this, I have yet to see a fashion show go as planned.

It was not for lack of excruciating planning of course. Every detail had been mapped to the last second months in advance and yet inevitably, someone impetrative would call in sick or a top investor would want to bring his six grandchildren backstage. Invariably, a model vomited on the runway or a make-up artist and hair stylist got into a fist fight.

It was what kept Amber's blood pressure skyrocketing and her heart rushing in her ears.

"Amber! Amber, you have an urgent phone call!"

Her assistant, Dana appeared, holding out one of the three cell phones she carried but Amber waved her away.

Every phone call was an urgent phone call. It was an occupational hazard.

"Not now, Dana. Can't you see we're T minus nineteen minutes?"

"Amber, you need to take – "

"Dana! I am up to my ears in disasters right now. Can you please deal with whatever it is? Is that not what I pay you the big bucks for?"

For a timeless second, a hush seemed to fall over the bustling backstage and inexplicably, Amber felt the hairs on her arms raise as she lifted her head.

She looked at Dana who shook her head quietly.

"What is it?" Amber breathed. "What happened?"

Dana visibly swallowed, lowering her kind, brown eyes through the lenses of her glasses.

She extended the phone further.

"It's your mother."

And Amber's world stopped.

Brooklyn, New York

"I'm looking for Leah Colville," Amber told the nurse. She drummed her fingers anxiously on the counter as the woman punched in the information and nodded.

"Room 717," she announced. "Just follow that hallway to the end."

Amber barely heard the last words as she flew down toward her mother's room.

It was slightly ajar and she pushed it open, her stomach flipping nervously.

"Mama?" she called softly. "Mama, are you awake?"

"Amber?"

She hurried inside the semi-private room, sliding the separating curtain aside.

Leah was the only one in the room but Amber knew that could change at the drop of a hat.

Oh mama, why didn't you say anything?

Her breath caught in her throat as she stared at her one virile mother, sunken in the bed, her face as white as the sterile sheets in which she lay.

Amber threw herself into her mother's arms gently.

"Oh mama," she whispered. "Why didn't you tell me it had gotten so bad?"

Leah made a dismissive sound with her tongue.

"You are a busy girl, Amber. The last thing you need is your old, sick mom crying in your ear about chemo treatments and hair loss. It's nothing you haven't heard a million times before."

Tears filled Amber's grey eyes but she hid them.

"I am never too busy for you," she scolded tenderly. "How long have you been like this?"

Leah sighed.

"Three weeks. The doctors are shocked I've hung on this long, kitten. It's only a matter of time..."

A stunning bolt of guilt almost brought Amber to her knees.

How could I not have known for three weeks? What kind of daughter am I?

"Don't talk like that!" Amber cried. "You're not going to..."

She trailed off as her voice caught in her throat.

"Shh, kitten. Don't cry now. We have both known that I have been living on borrowed time for a long while. God has been gracious enough to let me see you become successful and now I can go to the other side knowing you are secure."

Amber pursed her lips together, squeezing her mom's frail body.

"But I need you to do something for me," the older Colville woman continued and Amber raised her head.

"Anything, mama. Tell me what you need."

Leah studied her beautiful daughter's face for a long moment, reaching up to stroke her short, layered hair.

"Two things actually."

Amber stared at her expectantly.

"First, when I die, I need you to go to Pennsylvania and find my sister, Ruthie to let her know I've passed."

Amber stared at her uncomprehendingly.

"Your sister Ruthie?" she echoed. "Since when do you have a sister Ruthie?"

Leah offered her a weak smile.

"I have always had a sister, kitten."

Amber waited for her to elaborate but Leah seemed to have lost her strength suddenly.

"I'm tired, Amber," she murmured. "I would like to rest now."

"Yes, mama, of course," Amber replied, sitting up. "I will be right here when you wake up."

Leah patted her daughter's hand and smiled lovingly.

"The second thing I would like you to do it grow your hair long again. I miss those golden locks of yours."

Amber forced a smile through the tears in her eyes.

"I will do that mama. I will grow my hair and find Aunt Ruthie in Pennsylvania."

Leah nodded slowly, her eyes growing heavy.

"Just Ruthie, not Aunt Ruthie. You can find her in Eden, Pennsylvania. Ruthie Miller."

Amber watched with a trembling chin as her mother's eyes fell closed knowing that it was the last time she would ever see them open again.

Eden, Pennsylvania

Amber looked at the woman embarrassed.

"I'm afraid I don't know much more than what I've already told you," Amber admitted, wishing away the clerk's scornful scrutiny. "My mother asked me to find her sister here in Eden and I have no idea where to start."

The clerk gave her a look which was half bemused, half annoyed but she turned back to her computer.

"Ruth Miller," she sighed, shaking her head. "There has to be at least two dozen here and that's only the ones we have one record."

Amber blinked and stared at her.

"This is city hall, isn't it? Why wouldn't you have them on record? Do you have a lot of illegal immigrants here?"

Amber's question was sincere but the clerk's expression turned sardonic.

"You really are not from around here, are you?"

Amber swallowed her annoyance and forced a smile.

"No, ma'am. I am not. That is why any help you can give me would be greatly appreciated. Why would you not have someone on record?"

"This is Amish country, honey."

Amber suddenly felt foolish and she grinned sheepishly.

"Of course. Well, can you see if any of the Ruth Millers you have there have a sister named Leah?"

The clerk's red eyebrows rose almost to her hairline.

"Ruth and Leah Miller? Are you kidding me? You're definitely looking for an Amish family, sweetie."

"That can't be," Amber said shaking her head. "My mom wasn't Amish."

"Well, I can check but if it quacks like a duck..."

Again, her fingers flew over the keyboard and she raised an eyebrow.

"I have two Ruth Millers with a sibling named Leah."

She scrawled their telephone numbers onto a piece of paper for her.

"But I wouldn't get your hopes up, honey," the clerk told her as she held out the sheet. "My guess is that your Ruth Miller is somewhere in the countryside."

Amber stared at her helplessly.

"What do I do then?"

"If neither of these women is who you're seeking, I would start combing the districts."

Amber opened her mouth to ask what that meant but the older woman seemed irritated enough.

She closed her mouth and vowed to find someone else to help her find answers.

Instead, she thanked her and hurried out of the building, into the windy autumn day.

As she stood on the steps, looking down at the phone numbers in her hands, a memory flittered through her mind.

She had been about four years old and her mother pulled a long dress from a hope chest at the foot of the bed.

It had been just after Amber's father had died and Leah had been so melancholic, digging through old photos and keepsakes.

"That's an old dress, mama," Amber said, looking at the homespun fabric in awe.

"It is, kitten, yes," her mother agreed. "Would you like to try it on?"

"Yes please!" Amber cried and Leah had laughed, slipping the too large garment onto her small daughter.

The older Colville dug into the chest and removed a small white cap, placing it on the base of Amber's head.

"You look like a proper Amish girl now, *Liebchen*."

"What is an Amish girl, mama?"

"Greta!"

The voice was loud and almost directly in her ear, smashing her reverie into a million pieces.

Startled, Amber turned to look.

An Amish man stood behind her, his green eyes alight with hope as she met his stare.

"Greta, you've returned!" he said excitedly. "When did you come back to Eden?"

Amber shook her head.

"I'm sorry," she said kindly, still awed by the green of his irises. "You have me confused with someone else."

To her surprise, his brow furrowed and he scowled slightly.

"Are you playing a game?" he asked gruffly, his eyes narrowing. "You don't need to worry; I won't tell anyone I have seen you."

Amber's eyes widened and she wondered if she was in the middle of a gag.

She looked around for cameras but nothing seemed out of the ordinary.

"I really am sorry," she said again, continuing down the steps. "You have me mixed up with someone else. My name isn't Greta."

She hurried away before he could respond, leaving him staring after her.

As she made her way toward the street where her rental car waited, she glanced back uneasily at the attractive man, her heart racing.

That was strange, she thought, sliding into the driver's side.

But as she pulled away from the curb, she wondered if it was less strange and more fate.

Perhaps that man was God's way of telling her that she would find her long lost aunt inside the Amish community after all.

I guess it's time to start combing the districts, Amber thought wryly. *Whatever that means.*

She could not help but take one last peek at the man in her rear-view as she drove away. He remained standing on the steps, staring after her as if he expected her to return.

I hope he finds Greta, she thought wistfully. *He certainly seems to love her.*

"Abel, who was that?" Levi demanded, rushing up the steps of city hall to meet his brother. He peered in the direction which the car gone.

"Apparently no one," Abel muttered as he watched the small sports car zoom away from the center of town.

"From where I stood, it looked to be Greta Shetler and – "

"It was not," Abel snapped, cutting off his brother before another word could leave his lips.

Levi eyed him warily.

"You seem upset," he commented. "Hasn't that woman done enough damage to you without having you pine for her?"

"Let's not speak about her," Abel said between clenched teeth as he hurried down the steps. "We have errands to run."

Levi chuckled dryly.

"Well whoever she is, I would not mind seeing her again," Levi commented. Abel paused to give his brother a scathing look.

"She is an Englisher," he retorted. "You would do well to stay away from her."

"Why? Are you interested?" Levi mocked. "And I thought you were going to die longing for the shunned and shamed beauty of the district."

"You are speaking nonsense now, Levi," Abel chided. "If you can't speak normally, don't speak at all."

Abel didn't have to look over to know his brother was leering at him.

It seemed everyone in town had been ogling him since the day Greta had run off with the Englisher, leaving him at the altar after declaring she was pregnant with the Englisher's child.

And now she was back, pretending that she did not recognize him.

It was just another slap in the face after her ex-communication, almost two years earlier.

Has she come back to humiliate me further?

"Who was she if not Greta?" Levi demanded, obviously unwilling to leave the topic alone.

"You know you should not even be speaking her name," Abel snapped. "I don't know who that woman was."

"Then why did you run after her if you don't know her?"

Abel was growing angry with his brother's interrogation.

"Let us go our own way today. We can accomplish more that way."

Without permitting Levi an opportunity to answer, he rushed away, trying to leave his brother in his wake along with the painful memories of Greta.

After finding a quiet spot to park her car, Amber picked up her cell phone.

She tried both the phone numbers given to her by the clerk at city hall but as the woman had predicted, neither was the woman Amber sought.

Now I have to venture from district to district, she realized. She was not looking forward to the task; it seemed daunting but she knew she could not rest until she had honored her mother's wishes.

Instinctively, she reached up and touched her hair.

It had already begun to grow out some in the two months since Leah's passing and Amber was determined not to touch it.

As she drove the rental into the outskirts of Eden, the lush Pennsylvania hills fell into a smaller settlement of land and soon, she could see that she was inside the Amish district.

Almost immediately, a feeling of peace overcame her and she had to stop the car to admire the almost surreal beauty of the landscape around her.

She grabbed for her cell phone, snapping pictures as the horizon as the sun began to set over the lolling dales.

Suddenly, she heard the clopping of hooves as a wagon approached and Amber lowered her camera, watching in awe as a horse and cart ambled toward her.

In the front, a man and woman dressed in traditional Amish attire rode primly and Amber offered them a nervous smile, not knowing if she would be received with distain.

To her relief, they both returned her beam and the man slowed the beast.

"Are you lost, miss?" he asked politely and Amber shook her head.

"No...well maybe," she replied sheepishly. "I stopped to take a picture of the beautiful landscape but..."

She trailed off, suddenly embarrassed.

"I am afraid I'm on a bit of a wild goose chase," she confessed. They peered at her with curious eyes.

"Are you looking for someone's home?" the woman asked. "Perhaps we can direct you."

Amber opened her mouth to answer and then closed it.

"This is going to seem ridiculous," she muttered. "But I am looking for a woman named Ruthie Miller. Do you know her?"

The couple seemed slightly amused by the question and Amber was beginning to realize that was going to be a common response to her inquiry.

I wonder what it would be like to live in a place where everyone knew everyone else? I imagine there is a sense of security that accompanies that knowledge.

"I fear that we know several women by that name, miss. Can you tell us anything else about her?"

"She had a sister named Leah but they have been estranged for – "

Suddenly, Amber found it difficult to speak and she swallowed quickly as her voice broke.

"Have you had supper, miss?" the woman asked quietly. "Our farm is not far from here. It would be our pleasure to have you as our guest."

Amber looked up, terrified and shook her head.

"Oh no, I couldn't," she gulped. "But thank you."

The man smiled.

"It is considered very rude to refuse a supper invitation in Amish country," he informed her and Amber could see he was teasing her but all the same, she found herself nodding.

"That would be lovely," she breathed. "Thank you."

"You may follow us," the woman said, smiling.

Amber nodded and allowed them to pass before jumping back into her car.

What lovely people, she thought, her heart warming. The man on the steps of city hall had made her nervous and so far, he had been the only interaction she had with anyone in their culture.

But he did have lovely green eyes.

Amber steered the Chrysler into up the long drive of the pretty farmhouse, keeping a safe distance behind the kind strangers.

Slowly, she exited her car, suddenly aware of how strange was what she was doing.

Would I ever accept such an unexpected dinner invitation from random strangers in New York or Milan or Paris? Of course not. So why am I doing it here?

The answer was obvious; it felt right.

She was nowhere near any major city, designing clothes and fighting with stage hands or arguing with models.

It was like she had entered another world, another planet even where Amber Colville didn't exist and she was just a lost little girl, looking for the last family relation she had left in the world.

Does my Aunt Ruthie have children? Maybe I have cousins out there. Or should I say, in here.

"Come along, miss. It's growing cold without the sun shining down on us," the woman urged.

"My name is Amber," she volunteered as she was led into the house. "Amber Colville."

The wife smiled and nodded.

"That is a lovely name. I am Beth and that is my husband, Jeremiah Troyer."

"Pleased to meet you, Mr. and Mrs. Troyer," I said politely.

She smiled softly.

"We do not use such formalities here. You may call us Beth and Jeremiah," she said softly.

Amber blushed lightly and nodded.

"Only if you call me Amber," she agreed.

"Please, come and sit. Our boys should be along shortly. They have been commissioned with supper as Jeremiah and I were in town today."

"I see," she said, nodding. "But you are farmers?"

"Yes," Beth replied. "We grow wheat and barley. Our boys have recently acquired chickens but between you and I, Amber, I am rather fearful of their pecking beaks."

Amber chuckled with Jeremiah.

"There is no shame in having fears, Beth," her husband said, reassuringly. "I am certain even the English have fears."

Amber's smile broadened.

"Oh yes," she assured them. "More fears than I care to admit."

A sudden warmth flowed between them as they stood in a comfortable silence.

"Come along inside," Jeremiah said, shooing them from the foyer. "I will see about some cider. It is cooling in the shed. Abel just made a fresh batch."

"He's a good boy, our eldest," Beth murmured but Amber noticed a dark cloud cross over her eyes as if something occurred to her.

She stared at Amber, her mouth parting slightly.

"Is something wrong, Beth?" Amber asked, immediately concerned by her change of disposition.

The older woman shook her head.

"I will help Jeremiah with the cider. The barrel can be difficult to manage. Please, sit by the fire until we return."

She was gone before Amber could reply and she was abruptly filled with a small fission of alarm.

That was strange, she thought but she was ashamed of her suspicion. *Things are just done differently here than they are in the city. There's nothing strange about it.*

"*Mamm! Daed?*"

She turned her head as a man called out, poking his head into the sitting room where Amber had sunk into a wing chair.

He seemed to freeze as he looked at her.

"Hello," Amber volunteered. "I'm Amber Colville. Your parents have invited me for dinner."

A small smile appeared on the young man's lips and he stalked toward her, extending his hand.

"Levi Troyer," he announced. "You were in Eden today, were you not?"

Surprised, Amber nodded.

"Yes, I was at city hall, looking for information."

Levi's eyebrow raised.

"What sort of information?" he asked curiously, placing himself into the chair facing her.

Amber swallowed and shook her head.

"It's not really important," she said quickly. "I would rather not get into it right now."

Levi's blue eyes narrowed slightly.

"I can be a wonderful source of information," he told her. "If you ever feel like talking."

His meaning was unmistakable and Amber found herself amused and slightly intrigued by the forward speaking man.

"Thank you," she replied, laughing. "Perhaps after dinner. It's not a very cheerful supper conversation."

"Levi, why did you leave me alone to finish supper. I have – "

Amber turned toward the doorway again and her jaw dropped.

"Wh -what is she doing here?" the man gasped, looking accusingly at his brother. Levi jumped to his feet, grinning.

"It appears as thought *Mamm* and *Daed* have invited her over for supper. Amber, this is my brother, Abel."

Cautiously, Amber rose to her feet, unsure of how Abel would react to her as she recalled their previous encounter.

"Hello Abel," she said quietly. "Pleased to meet you."

She wasn't sure if she should extend her hand or not but she found herself once more staring into his impossibly green eyes as if hypnotized.

He did not immediately respond and Amber felt her heart sink slightly as he continued to stare at her.

"Forgive my brother," Levi interceded. Amber turned questioningly to him.

"He seems to think you look like someone he knew once a long time ago," Levi offered and Amber nodded slightly.

"I never said that," Abel grumbled but Amber felt that his gaze betrayed his words. He could not seem to pull his irises from her face as if trying to memorize every feature.

"There you are," Beth said, hurrying into the front room, a concerned expression on her face. She held out a glass for Amber.

"This is apple cider from the Bachman's orchid," she told Amber, smiling briefly. The older woman seemed to sense the tension in the room.

"I see you have met our sons, Abel and Levi," she continued as Amber accepted the cup. "What have you made for supper, boys? I am sure our guest is as hungry as your father."

"What did the doctor say, *Mamm*?" Abel asked suddenly, diverting his attention to his mother.

Beth's face turned pale and angry.

"Abel, that is hardly an appropriate question to ask before visitors. Go tend to supper," she snapped with a harshness Amber was sure was not customary.

Abel seemed contrite but he disappeared, bowing his head somewhat shamefully.

Amber felt a spark of apprehension in her stomach as she cast Beth a sidelong look.

Why did she go to the doctor? Is she ill? Does she have cancer like mama?

Amber bit on her lower lip and tried to push the image of her mother from her mind but it was more difficult than she wished.

"Are you all right, Amber?" Beth asked, her brow furrowing deeper as she watched the blonde's face crumble.

Amber tried to nod but a tear escaped her and slid down her cheek.

"I'm sorry," the younger woman told the others, quickly wiping the streak from her face. "I recently lost my mother and I was just thinking of her. Forgive me for my display."

Beth and Levi made a commiserating noise.

"Levi, go help your brother and leave the women to talk," Beth ordered. Levi rose without protest, leaving them alone in the front room.

"It is difficult to lose a parent," Beth said comfortingly. "I have lost both of mine."

Amber sighed.

"I am so sorry, Beth. My father also died when I was very young."

Beth leaned down to pat her hand soothingly and Amber found the gesture heartwarming.

I am a perfect stranger to her and yet she feels the need to comfort me. This place is like a television program. This isn't real life. This is a place where daughters would know that their mothers have been dying for weeks, not off running fashion shows in Italy.

"Supper is ready, *Mamm*, Amber," Levi called from the dining room and the women rose to join the others at the dinner table.

"We pray before eating, Amber. You are not required to join us," Jeremiah told her as she took a seat across from the Troyer brothers.

"I would be happy to join in your prayer if you'll have me," Amber replied. She pretended not to notice the look of appreciation shared by the family as she hung her head.

Jeremiah lead the prayer in Pennsylvania Dutch but Amber could catch some of the key words from the time she had spent in Munich.

"You still have not told us what you are doing in our district, Gre – ah, Amber," Levi piped up after they had loaded their plates with meat, vegetables, potatoes and bread.

Beth and Jeremiah looked up sharply while Abel's jaw tightened.

"Were you going to call me Greta also?" Amber asked, her eyes widening. Levi seemed embarrassed.

"You do bear an uncanny resemblance to her," he confessed.

"I did not notice," Beth interjected, eyeing her older son.

"Nor did I!" Jeremiah agreed and there was a finality in his tone. It was clear that the subject was to be dropped and Amber did not want to push the issue.

Nevertheless, she was fascinated by the fact she might have an Amish twin.

"I have come here looking for my mother's sister but I'm afraid I don't have much to go off. I don't even know if I'm looking in the right spot but my mom only told me about her before she died."

Beth looked up and smiled.

"We told Amber we would happily help her find her aunt but we would need to narrow the search somehow."

"What is her name?"

Amber was surprised it was Abel who asked the question.

"Ruthie Miller. Her sister, my mother, was Leah."

The table fell silent as the family appeared to rake their memories.

"Well, I can think of four women by that name. One is far too young to be your aunt, one is much too old and the other two have lived in the district all their lives without a sister named Leah," Jeremiah volunteered, chewing his fried steak pensively. "Have I forgotten someone?"

"No...I do not believe you have," Beth replied. She gazed at her boys.

"Any suggestions?"

Levi shrugged his shoulders.

"As Amber has said, there is no guarantee that this Ruthie Miller is from this district. Perhaps I could take her to the neighboring districts tomorrow and we could investigate further."

He beamed at her and Amber smiled back but she could not help her gaze from falling on the older Troyer brother.

He seemed to glower into his plate, unspeaking.

"That would be lovely," Amber said reluctantly, realizing that Abel was not about to volunteer his help.

Is he always so brooding or is it because I remind him of this Greta?

"It's settled then. Tomorrow I will take you in search of your aunt!" Levi said jovially.

Amber could not help but notice that he gently jabbed his brother in the ribs and she wondered if she hadn't put herself in the middle of a sibling rivalry.

Abel could not sleep and he lay on his back, arms folded across his chest.

"I can feel you breathing fire over there, Abe," Levi called mockingly through the dark. "Why are you so upset?"

"I'm not!" Abel denied but Levi only laughed.

"Why don't you just admit that you want to take Amber on her search tomorrow?"

"I do not," he replied hotly but as he said the words, he knew they were a lie.

He couldn't seem to get over the remarkable likeness Amber shared to Greta. It was as if *Gotte* had sent him a chance to get things right with Greta.

That's ridiculous. They are two different women. If Levi wishes to waste his time with an Englisher, let him do it.

"You truly are a fool," Levi sighed, sitting up. Abel turned his head to scowl at his brother in the moonlit room.

"You would know a fool to see one, brother," he snapped. "Stop talking and let me go to sleep."

Levi groaned.

"I only offered to take Amber tomorrow because I knew you wouldn't. You will pick her up at her hotel in Eden and take her."

"I will not!" Abel was insulted at the idea of stealing his brother's date. "She has agreed to go with you, not me."

"But she wants to go with you," Levi insisted. "She could not stop staring at you all through dinner. Didn't you notice?"

Abel had not.

"Of course you didn't notice. You were too busy sulking about Greta to notice the lovely woman yearning for you to look at her. I think Amber is *Gotte's* way of telling you that it is time to move on."

"What do you know?" Abel growled but in his heart, he felt a sliver of hope.

Is he just telling me that because he believes I have spent too much time pining over Greta or did Amber find me interesting?

"I know that if you don't act on this opportunity, I will give you no more second chances. I will pursue Amber myself."

Abel didn't answer but his heart sank at his brother's words.

Maybe this is a sign from Gotte. What harm can it do to take her tomorrow?

Amber felt a spark of happiness when she saw Abel at the reins the following morning in front of the Eden Resort and Suites.

"I hope you do not mind that I have come in my brother's place," Abel said, somewhat gruffly but Amber was already learning that it was shyness, not rudeness.

"I am very happy it was you," she replied earnestly, catching his eye.

A shiver coursed down her spine as he helped her onto the wagon and they made their way out of town toward the districts.

She found herself studying his handsome profile, taking in the fine shape of his nose and delicate bone structure.

"I hope that you will not be disappointed," Abel told her as they started their ride in silence.

Amber glanced at him in surprise, thinking that he had caught her staring at him.

She blushed and shook her head.

"I'm not disappointed in the least," she replied, lowering her eyes.

He shot her a sidelong look and gave her a lopsided smile.

"I meant that I hope you find your aunt," he explained. Amber turned bright red and cleared her throat in nervousness.

"Of course," she muttered, doubly ashamed.

She had almost forgotten the reason for their drive as if they were merely on a date.

Focus on the task at hand, she told herself.

Soon, they were in one of the neighboring districts and Abel proved to be a wonderful guide, finding a minister to question almost immediately.

They did not find anyone to match their description in the first two districts they visited but as they made their way into the third, it was growing late in the afternoon and Amber was growing disheartened.

"I'm beginning to think this is a lost cause," Amber confessed as they searched for the home of the deacon as directed by a young girl playing hopscotch.

Despite her mounting disappointment, she could not shake the idyllic beauty of their community.

I would give it all up to live here, she thought as they found Deacon Roth tending to his herb garden.

"Hello, Deacon," Abel called. "I am Abel Troyer and this is my friend, Amber. We have some questions for you if you have a moment."

The deacon looked up and nodded, smiling welcomingly.

"Of course," he agreed. "What can I help you with?"

"Deacon, have you a Ruthie Miller who lives here? She would be in her forties or fifties with an estranged sister named Leah?"

The elderly man's mouth parted and he stared at Amber for a long moment.

"Indeed," he murmured. "Are you Ruthie's daughter?"

Amber shook her head.

"No...I am Leah's daughter," Amber replied, glancing nervously at Abel. "Do you know them?"

The man nodded thoughtfully.

"Of course, I remember Leah. She never was baptized. She fell in love with an Englisher and married him when she was nineteen or so."

Amber nodded excitedly.

"Yes! Alexander Colville. That was my father," Amber gushed. "Is Ruthie still here?"

"No, child. Ruthie was married to a man named Samuel Miller but he died in a terrible accident not two years after the wedding. That was about a year after Leah had left the district."

Amber found her palms sweating and she wiped them on her jeans.

"Where did she go? Did my aunt leave the community too?"

The deacon chuckled.

"No, no. She eventually remarried and moved on to another district."

"Nearby?" Amber pressed, her excitement mounting.

I'm so close to finding your sister, mama! She thought, her heart racing.

"Yes, two districts across."

Abel's face turned confused.

"Closest to Eden?" he asked and the older man nodded.

"But that's our district," Abel murmured. A look of understanding crossed his face.

"Who did she marry when she moved?" he asked.

The deacon thought for a long moment, digging into the depth of his swiss cheese memory bank.

"Ah yes. David Shetler. As far as I know, they still live there but I confess, I am out of touch sometimes," Deacon Roth chortled.

Abel's face turned grey.

"Do you know these people, Abel?" Amber asked excitedly. "Do you know where I can find them?"

He looked at her, his face aghast.

"Yes," he whispered. "I know them. They are Greta's parents. You are Greta's cousin."

The ride back to Eden was long and quiet as Abel tried to gather his thoughts. To his relief, Amber did not push him to speak as if she could sense he needed the quiet.

Is this a cruel joke? Sending me a cousin of the woman who broke my heart? One who looks so much like her?

But as they continued the journey back, Abel suddenly realized that he had been blinded by Amber's outward appearance.

True, she looked like Greta with the solemn grey eyes as sunny blonde hair but how similar were the two really?

Greta could not seem to run away fast enough, sacrificing her own values to do so while Amber embraced her mother's home and heritage in tribute.

Greta was selfish and hurtful while Amber was kind and loving.

Greta was gone and Amber was right there beside him, waiting for him to speak, to make the next step.

"It is getting late," he finally told her. "I don't think it is wise to interrupt your aunt at this hour although I am certain she will be happy to see you, regardless of the time."

Amber nodded but he could see the sadness in her eyes.

"That's fine. I can find my own way there tomorrow," she replied, trying to sound cheerful. "But I appreciate all your help."

She turned her head quickly but he knew it was only so he wouldn't see the tears in her eyes.

He paused, searching for the next words to say.

Opening his mouth, his perfectly concocted statement flew into the air.

"I am hungry," he said instead.

Amber turned to glance at him.

"You're hungry?" she repeated. "Oh."

She wasn't quite sure what to make of the statement.

"Me too," she replied suddenly.

Their eyes met and they smiled.

"May I buy you dinner, Amber?" he asked her sweetly.

"Like a date?" she teased.

His smiled faded and he nodded solemnly.

"Exactly like a date," he replied.

END

LOVINA'S HEART

DEIDRA SCOTT

Chapter One

Lovina Miller took a deep breath as she reached up to pull a piece of laundry from the clothesline and put it in the basket at her feet. Above her head, a pair of bluebirds danced through the bright June sky, reminding her that summer was quickly approaching.

Summer. It was a time full of fresh starts and new beginnings.

Looking across the yard, Lovina watched David Yoder working with one of her brothers. Together, the two young men were struggling with their task, trying to break her *daed's* new horse.

Ach, just watching David sent a thrill of excitement through Lovina's heart. Although she had known him most of her life, there was something about him that could still put a spark inside of her, giving her the feeling that they had just met.

Growing up, Lovina had always dreamed of marrying David. It had just seemed natural to her. With their two houses located side-by-side, they had spent all of their childhood hours playing together in the creek that wound between their properties and climbing the big apple tree like little monkeys.

Lovina had decided early on that she and David would grow old together, spending their adult days raising babies and making a life within their Amish community.

Now that Lovina had turned eighteen-years-old, she felt like she was stuck in the midst of a waiting game, simply counting down the hours until David came forward to begin their relationship together.

Smiling to herself, Lovina basked in the realization that, as an adult, it was now time to watch her childhood dreams start to unfold.

"*Danki* for the help, David!" Lovina heard her father call out from the barn and looked up in time to see David waving goodbye to her family as he started across the yard.

Lovina felt her heart go aflutter when, rather than take the path back to his own parents' house, David veered closer to her own home and made a bee-line right for the clothesline where she was working.

"*Gut* afternoon, David!" Lovina called out, her voice seeming somewhat weak to her own ears.

Watching him come closer, Lovina couldn't help but marvel at how handsome her childhood friend had become. With a head-full of dark red hair and sparkling blue eyes, David had always looked like a cheerful storybook character; however, as he aged, he grew tall and muscular, his boyish looks transforming into that of a good-looking man.

"Hello there, Lovina," David called back, rolling down his sleeves as he walked along, "I tell you, that horse of your *daed's* nearly got me down this time!"

Lovina smiled as she pulled a pair of her brother's pants off of the laundry line and tossed them in the basket, "I guess we should consider ourselves glad to have such a good horse-breaker living so near-by."

To her surprise, David's face suddenly seemed to darken. Taking a deep breath, he reached up and put one hand on the clothesline, "Actually, Lovina, I wanted to talk to you about that."

Although Lovina had hoped that David would want to talk to her alone, she could already tell that his news wasn't going to be what she had wanted to hear.

"Lovina," David looked out across the fields, "Ever since you had your birthday, I'd been hoping..." his voice trailed off and he gave a shrug, "Well, nothing I'd hoped for is going to work out this summer." Standing up taller, he announced, "My uncle from Indiana wrote telling about the need for a good horse-trainer in his community. I agreed to go help for the next three months...I'll be home in time to help my dad get started on the harvest."

Lovina felt her heart drop in her chest. The idea that David would leave had never entered her mind. Even though it was only for three months, it felt like it might as well be three years.

"*Ach*, Lovina, don't be so sad," David reached out and placed his hand on her arm, "I'll be back – I promise. Kentucky is my home...I sure don't have any plans to run off for good."

Something about having his hand on her arm made the pain a little more bearable. Looking up, Lovina met David's tender gaze with her own.

"When I come back..." David took a deep breath and kicked at a clump of grass with his foot. It was strange to see him so uncomfortable – David was usually one to be bold and daring, willing to say whatever was necessary.

"When I come back, I hope we can spend more time together," David managed to say, "Seems like we've grown apart over the years, and I'm ready for that to end."

Lovina couldn't stop the smile that spread across her face, "And maybe not be climbing trees this time?" She added.

David laughed, "Of course we'll be climbing trees again!" He teased.

Growing more sober, he lifted his hand and ran it gently across her cheek, "I'll see you in three months, 'Vina."

Three months. As she watched him walk away and back to his parents' farm across the creek, Lovina took a deep breath and tried to still her thumping heart. Three months was a long time – she was just glad that she had those tender moments to cling to during the summer that stretched out before her.

Chapter Two

Taking a deep breath, David watched out the passenger window as the driver he had hired took him farther and farther from his home in Kentucky and on toward his Uncle Amos' house in Indiana.

"Are you nervous about leaving home for so long?" David's paid driver, Mr. Simpson asked, as he flipped his turn signal on and proceeded toward Uncle Amos' house.

David shook his head and laughed, "*Ach*, no, not nervous."

"Anxious to get away from your parents?" Mr. Simpson asked with a chuckle.

"No, nothing like that." David assured him, "Just glad to be helping my uncle and the people in his community."

Leaning his head back against the headrest of the seat, David closed his eyes and thought about Mr. Simpson's question.

Was he glad to be getting away from his parents? Although he had been quick to assure his driver that wasn't he case, David wasn't so certain himself. To be completely honest, David wasn't a bit sorry to be leaving for the summer. While he had always loved his home and his family, David relished the chance to get away.

Since David had been a little boy, he had always known what was expected of him. He was going to settle down, buy a piece of property close to his parents, and marry Lovina Miller. It wasn't a bad plan at all, but it seemed so boring and dull. Deep in his heart, David had always dreamed of excitement and adventure. Maybe his trip to Indiana would finally provide him with a chance to enjoy his freedom before he settled down for good.

David's driver took him straight to Uncle Amos' house, helped him unload his bags, and then left him to head back to Kentucky.

Uncle Amos and his entire family were happy to welcome David to their home. Uncle Amos explained that everyone in the community could use his horse breaking services and that they would be bringing their horses to his house so that David could train them. Uncle Amos also said that, during David's spare time he could help the family out in the dry goods store they had located in a small shed next to the road.

"I'll take you out to the store now, so that I can show you what kind of work you can do out there." Uncle Amos suggested once David had put his clothes away in the spare bedroom.

Leading David across the yard, Uncle Amos explained, "Of course, I will pay you for helping in the store...and you can also have all the money for training the horses."

David shook his head, "*Ach,* that's too much, Uncle Amos. I'm happy to have the chance to help out."

Uncle Amos chuckled and reached out to give David a slap on the back, "Now, now, don't go talking like that. I'm sure a handsome young man like you should be saving back to buy a nice farm and making plans for the future. I'd dare say that some pretty girl back home has caught your eye."

David gave a shrug, not too anxious to think about his future, "Nothing set in stone just yet."

The graveled lane ended and the two men found themselves standing side-by-side outside of the dry goods store. Reaching out, Uncle Amos pushed the door open, revealing a building with shelves full of baking supplies, canned goods, and some craft items.

"Hannah!" Uncle Amos called out, as he led David through the small building, "Hannah!"

"I'm over here," a soft voice returned.

Turning the corner around one of the shelves, they found a young Amish woman on her knees, busy stacking bags of flour.

"Hannah, I want you to meet my nephew, David," Uncle Amos announced, "David, this is Hannah – she is my wife's cousin and she's helping us out in the store this summer."

Hannah pulled herself to her feet and turned to stare up at David with large, blue eyes. Wisps of dark hair had escaped her prayer *kapp,* making a sort of halo around her face.

Just looking at her, David felt his heart give a leap. She was so unexpectedly beautiful in a dark, mysterious way.

"*Gut* to meet you, David," Hannah replied timidly.

"David is likely to be helping out in the store when he isn't working with the horses," Uncle Amos explained. Giving David a pat on the arm, he motioned toward the back room, "Come on, I want to show you where I store the bulk supplies."

As David followed his uncle, he had a hard time even listening to what was being said. His mind was still mesmerized by the beautiful and timid young lady he had just met. David could hardly wait to get to know and learn more about Hannah.

Lovina sat on the edge of her bed, looking out across the fields of farmland through her bedroom window. Knowing that David was no longer in the house next-door left a hollow emptiness in Lovina's heart. In her eighteen-years, she had never gone a summer without seeing David.

Lovina tired to imagine what her sweet friend was doing at that moment. Did he realize how much she was thinking of him? Did he miss her at all?

Lovina closed her eyes and took a deep breath, "Dear God," she whispered into the darkness, "Please, bring the man that I love back to me."

Chapter Three

David carefully guided his uncle's buggy down the road. It was only his second day in Indiana and work was already starting to pick up; however, Uncle Amos had sent him to town to pick up some nails for a woodworking project he was doing in the barn.

The summer afternoon sun shone down on David and the warmth of the breeze put a smile on his face. David was enjoying his time away from home and, although he had not had many opportunities to spend time with Hannah, he had hopes that would change eventually.

The buggy suddenly took a lung, pulling David out of his thoughts.

"Woah, boy! Woah!" David pulled tightly on the reigns, unsure of what was happening to the buggy. Carefully guiding the horse to the side of the road, he jumped down from his seat and looked over the situation.

Something was wrong with the front buggy wheel. Grabbing a hold of it, David gave it a wiggle, trying to determine if it could keep going.

Pulling off his straw hat, David slapped it against his leg in frustration. He couldn't get to town on that wheel and he didn't think he could make it back to his uncle's house either.

The clipping of oncoming horse hooves made David stand up straighter and wave desperately at the approaching buggy.

The driver was a single Amish man. As soon as David caught his attention, the other driver pulled his buggy to the side of the road behind David.

"Hi there!" David greeted with a smile as he watched the other Amish man get off his buggy and start toward him, "Boy, I sure am glad to see you!" Sticking out a hand, he announced, "I'm David Yoder. I'm staying with my Uncle Amos Yoder – you probably know him."

The stranger nodded and simply said, "I'm Luke Christner." Taking a deep breath, he walked over to the buggy and squatted down to inspect the wheel.

"Looks like this is busted good," he announced, pushing his hat back on his head and reaching up to wipe some sweat from his brow.

David groaned, "I was afraid of that."

Standing to his feet, Luke continued, "I'm afraid you shouldn't drive it any farther than just a few feet or you'll end up wrecking or destroying your entire buggy." With a slight smirk, Luke added, "Lucky for you, this is my parents' drive right up ahead. And I just happen to work on buggies for a living."

David's eyes got large and he let out a huge sigh, "Oh, *gut*! Do you think that you could help me out?"

Luke nodded, "Sure thing. Just lead your buggy down to my workshop. I'll have her fixed up in just a bit."

True to his word, Luke had the buggy wheel fixed within an hour.

David stayed by the young man who had rescued him and worked to fill him in on all the details about his life, his home, and his family. Luke, who seemed to be more reserved, was happy to listen and donate very few details of his own.

"How much do I owe you?" David asked as Luke put the repaired wheel back on his buggy.

Luke gave a shrug as he secured the wheel in place, "Nothing. Consider it a welcome present. Maybe you can help me with one of my horses one day this summer."

"*Ach*," David raised an eyebrow, "I can't let you do that. I took some time you could have been working on other projects..."

Before he could finished, Luke started shaking his head, "No, no you didn't," he assured David as he stood up straight, "Honestly, I didn't have any other work for today." Sighing deeply, he announced, "As badly as we need a horse trainer in this area, we do not need any kind of buggy work. Jobs around here are scarce, David. I was glad to help."

David pondered Luke's statement for a moment. As an idea entered his mind, a broad smile spread across his face, "Listen, Luke! You may not be needed here, but you sure would be in my community! How would you feel about going to Kentucky to spend the summer with my family? It would sure help them out while I'm gone, and you could earn money doing buggy repairs and carpentry work!"

Luke was silent, obviously studying David's suggestion. Finally, with a shrug, he announced, "*Jah* – I don't see why that wouldn't be great. *Danki*, David."

The entire plan made David's face light up like that of a little boy. Grinning from ear-to-ear, he grabbed his new friend's hand in a shake and started making plans to get Luke back to Kentucky.

Chapter Four

Lovina reached up to wipe some sweat from her forehead as she took a break from chopping weeds out of the row of green beans. Despite all her hard work, the weeds were quickly starting to overtake the plants.

David had now been gone two weeks, and Lovina had yet to hear anything from him. His absence made her sad and she wished for all she was worth that she would receive a letter.

Glancing across the field toward his house, she thought of all the times they had snuck away from their chores and played together instead.

To her surprise, Lovina saw a young man approaching her. Could it be...? Lovina's heart dropped as he drew closer. Although she had hoped that it was David, she instantly realized that her eyes had been playing tricks on her. This stranger was even taller than her dear childhood friend and slightly thinner.

"Hullo," Lovina called out as he continued to draw closer.

"Hullo," the stranger returned, his voice deep and almost mysterious, "Are you Lovina Miller?"

Lovina stood up straighter and adjusted her prayer *kapp*, "That would be me. Do I know you?"

The stranger shook his head, "No, you don't." Now he was so close that Lovina was able to get a good look at him. This strange Amish man looked to be in his early twenties, but he seemed more mature. His brown hair was so dark it was almost black, and his eyes a dark color chocolate. Just looking at him made Lovina take a deep breath of surprise. *Ach*, it was hard to remember a time that she had ever seen such a *gut*-looking man!

"I'm Luke Christner. I know your friend, David, and I'm staying with his family until he returns." Glancing toward her house, Luke asked, "Is your *daed* at home? The Yoders told me that he has a construction crew and I'd like a job."

Lovina felt so out of sorts, she wasn't sure what to do. Looking down at her bare feet, she tried to gather her composure. Taking a deep breath, she said, "*Nee*, my *daed* isn't home from work yet, but we're expecting him any minute. If you'd like to wait in the house, my *mamm* can give you some fresh lemonade and cookies."

Luke glanced from the house back to Lovina and then shrugged, "If you don't mind, I'll just stay out here. Looks like you could use some help." Grabbing for an extra hoe, Luke set to work, removing the pesky weeds from among the rows of bean plants.

There was something about Luke that made Lovina feel uncertain about everything. He was a good help in the garden, but she certainly would have felt more at-ease without him. On the other hand, she dreaded him leaving once her father got home from work. Just being near him made her feel things that she had never experienced – she found herself overwhelmed by a sort of giddiness that sprung up from deep within. Although Lovina had always been a talker, she suddenly seemed almost speechless.

"You don't have to do this," Lovina assured him.

Luke simply set his jaw and turned to look at her with his brooding, dark eyes, "I don't have to...but I want to."

Lovina felt weak in the knees, as if she might keel right over. Taking a deep breath, she tried to stead herself.

Suddenly, she found herself a little glad that David was going to be gone for the summer. As quickly as the thought flitted through her mind, she pushed it away; however, just the realization that she could think such a thing left Lovina questioning everything about the future.

David washed his hands in a pail of water that had been set out by the barn, preparing himself for the evening meal. Inside the house, Aunt Miriam was putting the finishing touches on a pot of homemade chili with the help of three of David's cousins.

True to Uncle Amos' word, in the time that David had spent in Indiana he had already been so busy, he hardly had time to even think about being at home.

Wiping his clean hands on a towel, David glanced across the acres of land that his uncle owned. There, in the glowing darkness of the evening, he could make out the form of a young woman walking near the pond.

Hannah.

David had learned to recognize her from a distance. Even though it would be hard to distinguish her from any other Amish woman from so far away, David could pick Hannah out because she was always alone. It seemed like she carried an air of sadness with her, wherever she went.

Taking a deep breath, David stepped out of the barn and started the short walk to the pond.

"Hi there," David called out as he drew near to Hannah.

The young woman looked up at him and gave a sad smile.

"What are you doing?"

Hannah gave a shrug and pulled her black shawl tighter against her shoulders, "I just felt like a walk," she explained.

David stepped up next to her side, "It must be sort of lonely to walk all alone."

Hannah shrugged again, "I'm used to being alone."

David *thought* over his childhood and how little time he had ever spent just to himself. There were always siblings to play with, other Amish children to enjoy at events, and Lovina. Lovina had always been there for him.

Just the thought of his old friend's name sent a nagging sense of guilt through his mind.

Hadn't he promised Lovina that, when he got home, things would be different? Hadn't he promised that they would spend time together? So, what was he doing, trying to get closer to Hannah?

"David..." Hannah's soft voice brought him out of his thoughts, "Are you all right, David? I've never seen you so solemn and quiet."

David looked up at her in surprise, his face breaking out in a broad grin, "Oh, *jah*, I'm fine. I was just thinking is all."

"I didn't know you were able to do that...you know, think without saying what was going through your mind." Although Hannah's words were haughty, David *looked* up in time to catch a teasing smile cross her lips. It was the first time he had ever seen her smile and, something about it made him want to see it a thousand times more.

"Maybe it's too much time around you," David suggested, "Because I don't think you ever say anything much at all."

Hannah's tender smirk turned into a broad smile and David was, once again, captivated by her charm.

Reaching out, he gently took her elbow in his hand, "Would you do me the honor of letting me walk with ya tonight?"

Hannah was silent for a moment, studying David for all that he was worth. Finally, she nodded slowly and said, "*Jah* – I suppose that might be nice."

Chapter Five

Just as David had predicted, it was easy for Luke to find work in Kentucky. He not only spent his afternoons working on buggies in the Yoder's empty shed, but also joined the carpentry work crew lead by Lovina's father.

Lovina wasn't exactly sure how it happened, but it seemed that she and Luke were constantly thrown in the paths of one another. Lovina tried to convince herself that it was merely a coincidence, but she had to admit that it was more than that.

The longer David was gone, the less she was thinking about him and the more she was thinking about Luke.

When he wasn't busy with work, Luke frequently dropped by to help Lovina in the garden; although he wasn't a talker, there was something about his calm attitude that left Lovina yearning for more time with him.

One evening, Lovina baked a plate of her famous homemade ginger snap cookies and decided to take a few across the creek as a thank you for Luke's help in the garden.

Knocking on the shed door, she cautiously pushed it open, cheerfully announcing, "Hello! Luke! Are ya in here?"

"*Jah*, I'm here," Luke replied.

There he was, standing next to a work bench with a busted buggy wheel laid out in front of him.

"Hi there!" Lovina greeted him, suddenly feeling unsure of herself and terribly bashful, "I thought I might bring you something." Placing the plate of cookies on the work table, she watched Luke eyeball them before picking one up and putting it in his mouth.

"It's just a thank you for all the help you've been giving me," she explained.

Luke raised his eyebrows and nodded as he swallowed, "*Danki* – they're very good. You're a good baker, Lovina."

Lovina felt her heart skip a beat with his compliment. Looking at the work he was doing, she added, "Looks like you've got quite a few talents of your own."

Reaching for another cookie, Luke gave a shrug, "I keep busy for sure....but that's a good thing. I'm always thankful for the money."

Leaning back against the table, Lovina studied him in the growing darkness, "Saving back for a farm of your own?"

Luke stared straight at his work and shook his head, "No. I'm going to give my money to help out my family. I have no need of a place of my own."

"Don't you ever hope to get married and have a family?"

Luke shook his head slowly, "I'm afraid all of my dreams are gone. I plan to be alone forever."

His words broke Lovina's heart. Although he tried to sound resolved, it was easy to hear the pain in his voice.

"*Ach*, Luke," she managed to whisper with a smile, "Don't say that. You never know what might happen."

Luke took in a deep breath and then let it out slowly. Looking up to meet Lovina's eyes, he studied her for what seemed minutes before asking, "What about you? Do you think that you could ever love someone like me?"

His question took Lovina by such surprise that she almost fell over. Her eyes growing large, she looked down at the floor, her heart flooded by a million different emotions.

"I...I...Luke..." Lovina's voice was trailing in every direction but her words were making no sense at all.

"Lovina," Reaching out, Luke put his hand on top of hers, "Would you consider going with me to the singing after church this weekend?"

It felt like Lovina would not be able to breath, so many decisions were running helter-skelter through her mind. Almost a surprise to herself, she heard her voice say, "Sure. I don't see why not."

Although David had been staying busy with the horses, he still managed to make some time to help out in the store. With a beautiful girl like Hannah there, he had to find time to spend with her.

One afternoon they had received a large order of supplies and were hurrying to put them on the shelves before it would be too dark to see, even by the glow of the lantern.

"*Ach*, this is a job!" David grumbled as he hurried to put some bags of flour in their place on a shelf, "Of course this would just happen to be the night that Uncle Amos and his entire family went visiting...leaving you and me to do all the work."

Hannah smiled and shook her head, "David, you complain so much. I don't mind the work. Work keeps me busy...work keeps my mind off of...other things."

Suddenly interested, David looked up in surprise. Maybe he would finally have a chance to hear some of the secrets that were hidden away behind this mysterious girl's sad blue eyes.

"What other things?" David asked.

Hannah shrugged as she ran her fingers over a bag of sugar, "Disappointments...heartbreaks...bad decisions."

Hannah went silent, assuring David that he would hear no more of her story, but then she surprised him when she went on to clear her throat and say, "I had a boyfriend...a fiancé even."

As the words came pouring out of her mouth, it was easy to see that they were tearing her apart. Hannah closed her eyes and continued, "But things didn't work out. We were engaged but...well, I was filled with so many uncertainties. I called off the wedding before it was even announced in church. I didn't mean to end everything with him – I just needed more time to think. But I'm afraid he took it as an outright rejection. And now, I'll never have a chance with him again," Hannah reached up to wipe away the tears that were threatening to overwhelm her, "*Ach*, David, it almost breaks my heart to talk about it. I have destroyed all my chances for happiness."

Looking at her in the light of the lantern, her face clouded over with pain and tears gathering in her eyes, David felt totally broken for her. Pulling himself to his feet, he stood up straight and stepped closer to her, putting a hand on her thin shoulder.

"Hannah," he whispered her name with all the tenderness that he had been storing in his heart, "Dear Hannah...you still have a thousand chances for happiness." Reaching up, he took his thumb and brushed a tear off of her cheek.

Hannah took a deep breath and let it out slowly. Looking at him in surprise, she simply whispered, "*Danki*, David." Then she squared her shoulders and announced, "Let's get back to work."

Chapter Six

Over the next few days, David and Hannah had little time to spend together. He looked forward to ever chance he had to see her. Although their friendship had not had time to progress, David felt confident that over the rest of the summer he could easily earn himself a special place in Hannah's lonely heart.

One afternoon, David had finally found a chance to work in the dry goods store alongside Hannah when one of his cousins came rushing into the shed with a letter in his outstretched hand.

"David," the little cousin called out, "You got some mail!"

Taking the letter, David quickly recognized the handwriting as that of his younger sister, Lydia.

Ripping the seal open, David pulled out the letter, unsure why his teenage sister would even take the time to write him.

Dear David,

I don't want to bother you while you're gone, but I need to let you know something important. I've always thought that you and Lovina had something special together, although I'm not sure if you had any kind of plans for the future or an agreement. While you've been gone, Lovina has taken a spark to the very man you sent here to work – Luke Christner. Seems like they're seeing each other almost every day and last night I overheard him invite her to the singing Sunday night. She agreed to go with him.

I don't mean to stick my nose in where it doesn't belong, but I know that you were always sweet on Lovina and just thought you should know.

Your sister,

Lydia

"*Ach*," David read over the letter and then reread it again, his heart suddenly dropping into his stomach.

Lovina – with Luke? A multitude of emotions suddenly assailed David. He found himself so frustrated, almost angry at Luke for stealing his girl. How dare Luke go to David's own home and try to take the woman he loved away from him? David was hurt, so hurt, by Lovina's decision to move forward with a relationship with someone else. But, worst of all, David felt incredible guilt and sadness.

Deep in his heart, David realized that it was his own fault that Lovina and Luke were growing close. In all the time that David had been in Indiana, he had never taken the time to even write his childhood sweetheart a letter – he had just always taken for granted that she would be there for him when he returned.

While he had been busy pursing a friendship with Hannah, he had never thought that Lovina might be looking at someone else.

Reaching up, David rubbed his hand across his face, trying to gather his wits and decide what to do next.

"What is wrong, David?" Hannah asked softly as she stepped up next to him.

David balled his free hand up into a fist, fighting the urge to destroy the letter he had just received. Passing it to Hannah, he quickly explained, "I don't know how to tell you this, Hannah, but Lovina...well, she and I have always been friends. I don't mean to have led you astray in any way because I have liked you since the day we met but this..." David couldn't go on.

Hannah took the letter in her own hands and read it slowly, her eyes growing large as she went over the message again and again.

"David," she managed to breath softly, "What are you going to do?"

David brushed his hand through his hair as memories of Lovina ran across his mind, "I don't know. I just don't know." Turning, he gave the floor a hard kick with the toe of his boot.

"David," Hannah took a deep breath and shook her head slowly, "I hate to say this, but you know that we aren't meant to be together. No matter how happy we might have both been to pretend...it just isn't so. You have made my summer much more enjoyable...but it's time to get back to our real lives."

David looked down at his feet. He wanted to fight her words; he hated the idea of giving Hannah up completely. But, when he thought of his dear Lovina...he knew that he couldn't live without her.

"Go to her, David!" Hannah exclaimed, "Go to Lovina and let her know that you love her."

Taking a deep breath, David nodded his head, "I'll go call a driver right now."

Chapter Seven

David sat in the passenger seat of the truck, half-heartedly listening as his driver talked incessantly during the long trip back home. Looking out the window, David watched the scenery slowly change from the flat Amish country of Indiana to the rolling hills of Kentucky.

With each mile that passed, it seemed that David got even more nervous about his future with Lovina.

When he first started home, he had been certain that she would be glad to see him but now...well, the closer he got to her, the less sure he became. Maybe she had truly fallen for Luke and she wouldn't want to even see him. Maybe David had blown his one and only chance for true love with the only girl he ever truly cared for.

Lovina had just filled up a bucket of water and got down on her knees to scrub the kitchen floor with a scrub brush when she heard a truck pull up in the front yard.

Ach, Lovina thought to herself as she plunged her hands down into the soapy water, *Daed must have visitors.*

It was Saturday afternoon and Lovina found her mind plagued with thoughts of Luke and their upcoming date. Although she truly enjoyed spending time with him, there was something about agreeing to go on a date with him that put her mind entirely in a tizzy. As much as she liked Luke and was attracted to him, Lovina battled thoughts of David – it seemed so sad to be turning her back on their relationship with each other.

But, she reasoned to herself, when she thought back on it, she and David had never had a true relationship. Sure, he had always been a good friend to her, but it seemed that was all things were to ever be. Since he left for Indiana, she had not heard a word from him and, as sad as she was to admit it, she was starting to wonder if he would ever come home at all.

"Lovina."

The voice seemed to come out of no where. Lovina looked up in surprise, wondering if she was truly hearing a person or if it was her own imagination.

There, standing in the doorway to the kitchen, was David himself.

"David!" Lovina managed to breathe as she struggled to pull herself to her feet, "Oh, David...is that really you?"

In an instant, David had bridged the space between them. He came right to her side, nearly knocking her bucket of soapy water over in his hurry.

"Lovina," David managed to say, somewhat louder this time, "Lovina..." he seemed to want to say more, but acted as if he couldn't find the words. Reaching out, he grabbed Lovina and gathered her into his arms.

To Lovina, everything felt like a crazy dream. Pressed firmly against her old friend's body, all thoughts of Luke vanished from her mind as she let David hold her like a little girl.

"Lovina," David pulled back only long enough to kiss her on the mouth, "Lovina, I have been a total moron. I am so sorry!"

"David," Lovina managed to say as she tried to catch her breath, "David...what has happened?"

David stepped back as he struggled to gather his composure. Reaching up, he wiped away at tears that threatened to overtake him.

"Lovina," he reached out and held her hands in his own, "I have been so ignorant. I left home, anxious to find adventure and experience new things...and I almost lost the one thing that means the most to me in the world – you."

Lovina felt her heart start to melt as David poured out his soul to her, "Lovina, I love you. I love you more than I ever realized. I thought that Uncle Amos was giving me a chance to experience adventure but I think it was actually the good Lord allowing me the opportunity to realize how much I love you. Please, Lovina...I don't want to wait any longer. Say that you will marry me!"

There had never been anything that Lovina wanted more. In that instant, it felt like all of her hopes and dreams were finally coming true.

Luke.

The name entered her mind suddenly and it felt like the life was drained right out of her. Oh, but hadn't she already led him to believe that she cared for him? Hadn't she already agreed to go out on a date with him this very weekend?

"David," Lovina squeezed her dear friend's hands tightly as she looked for the right words to share her news, "David. I have been a foolish girl."

"And I have been a foolish man," David was quick to add.

Lovina smiled and shook her head, "Perhaps we've both been foolish…"

Her words were cut short as the sound of an approaching vehicle brought them both from their thoughts.

Glancing out the window, they watched together as a strange car stopped in front of the house and let out a passenger.

David felt his heart sink when he saw the visitor who was getting out of the strange car.

It was Hannah.

David thought that she had understood. What was she doing…following him all the way to Kentucky of all places? Hadn't she been the one who had said that their relationship wasn't going to work and even pushed him to return to Lovina? What was she doing here now?

David battled the urge to run forward and stop her before she could get to the house. Turning to Lovina, he struggled to find the words to explain what was surely about to come.

"Lovina…" he hurried to say, "While I was gone, I was an idiot. I hate telling you this more than you will ever know, but I got involved with a girl from Indiana. We never started to court, but we were heading in that direction when I heard that you and Luke had begun a relationship…."

As the words poured from his mouth, David watched Lovina's face turn ashen and then red with shame.

"You already know about Luke?" She managed to whisper.

David nodded his head, "That was the wake-up call I needed. That was what I needed to bring me back home. I never want to risk losing you again, Lovina!"

Lovina started to wipe tears away from her eyes, "David, I don't want to lose you either! But what you heard is true. Luke and I have grown close and are on the verge of starting a relationship. I was so foolish, David, but I was afraid I had lost you and now I don't know what to do..."

In the other room, they could hear a knock on the front door.

Wiping at her eyes, Lovina hurried to go open it with David trailing close behind. When she opened the door, Hannah was standing on the front porch, a determined look in her blue eyes.

"I need to talk to David," she announced, looking from Lovina to David.

"David," she took a deep breath, "I need to go to your house...I need to see Luke."

Luke? David was more confused than ever. Cocking his head to one side, he tried to understand where this strange twist came into play.

"You don't have to look far," the deep voice of Luke spoke out and they all turned in surprise to find that he had come up on the porch and was standing just out of view.

"Hannah," as he said the name, his voice seemed to fill with a strange sort of pain.

"*Ach*, Luke..." Hannah looked down at her black shoes as if she couldn't hold his gaze, "I have been wanting to talk to you."

Luke shook his head sadly, "I can't imagine what we would have to say to each other now."

"Luke...you know that I am a very shy girl," Hannah said in a shaky voice, "And I have let my fear get the better of me far too many times. I almost let it destroy what we had together. But Luke...I can't let that happen."

David's eyes got large as he realized that Luke must be the ex-beau that Hannah had told him about.

"I love you, Luke," Hannah announced resolutely, "I love you and I still want to be your wife...if you can ever find it in your heart to have me."

David watched Luke and held his breath, hoping that he would agree.

Stepping forward, Luke reached out and took Hannah in his arms, "I love you too, Hannah!" He exclaimed as he cupped her face in his hands, "I have always loved you and I always will." Turning to look at Lovina, he quickly tried to explain, "Lovina, I hope that you understand..."

Lovina smiled broadly as she wrapped her arms around David's waist, "It is fine, Luke. I think that things are exactly the way that they are supposed to be!"

Epilogue

Standing together at the kitchen sink, Lovina and David watched as a group of children played outside in their front yard.

"Look at those crazy things," Lovina muttered as she noticed her daughter trying to climb a tree.

"Just like us when we were little," David announced.

Lovina looked up at him and smirked, "*Jah* – and I think our little girl might have a crush on the neighbor boy, as well."

David and Lovina had now been married for ten years and had three children of their own. It had been a double wedding shared with Hannah and Luke, who decided to move to Kentucky so that Luke would continue to enjoy a steady stream of work.

David and Lovina had built their house behind his parents' place and, to their surprise, Hannah and Luke had bought a piece of farm land right across the creek.

Their children played together and it wouldn't be any surprise if someday those same children would grow up to marry one another.

David smiled broadly and gathered his wife up in his arms.

"I'm glad I went to Indiana that summer," he announced as he reached out to push a strand of her brown hair back from her face, "Because that summer showed me how much I need you in my life."

Bending over, he gave her a gentle kiss.

Life truly was as David and Lovina had always imagined it – and they were happier than they ever could have guessed possible.

THE END